# Ian and the Padre

### A Story By
### James F. McCarthy

**Edited by Tamara Pugh**

**Illustrations by Alysia Dorhout**

**Cover by Thomas Raasio**

**Outskirts Press, Inc.**
**Denver, Colorado**

Ian and the Padre
All Rights Reserved.
Copyright © 2010 James F. McCarthy
Edited by Tamara Pugh
Illustrations by Alysia Dorhout
v4.0

Outskirts Press, Inc.
http://www.outskirtspress.com

ISBN: 978-1-4327-5387-0

Outskirts Press and the "OP" logo are trademarks belonging to Outskirts Press, Inc.

PRINTED IN THE UNITED STATES OF AMERICA

# Chapter 1

# "Father Bill"

This story brings together two persons from completely different backgrounds. They meet each other in Antrim Junction, a small town in northwestern Michigan's lower peninsula. Much to the surprise of each of them, Antrim Junction is a town of deep Scottish heritage. Antrim Junction is also beset with a rampant numbers racket.

Father William MacKenzie, a newly ordained Catholic priest is sitting in the ante room of Bishop Sullivan's house in Evart, Michigan. He is giving in to some self pride and vanity as he is admiring his newly printed calling cards: "Reverend Father William MacKenzie". He is suitably impressed with his new found personal importance, as he considers being a dynamic new element in the Catholic church.

Bill is wondering what is keeping Bishop Sullivan, after all, it is twenty minutes past the time set for this interview. His personal tension is mounting as time presses on. Bill's mind is considering a recurrent question: "Why didn't I receive my assignment before the ordination as the other new priests did? What will the Bishop tell me? What will be my assignment? Could I be going to a parish of such importance that Bishop Sullivan will personally direct the event? If this is a really important job, then, I will surely have to have the calling cards reprinted to reflect the status of my new job."

Again, the thought that Bishop Sullivan is keeping him waiting crosses through his mind. "What is keeping the Bishop?"

After an eternity of waiting, Father Lewis came into the ante room to announce that it was time to go inside for his interview with Bishop Sullivan. Father Lewis leads the way down the hallway to the Episcopal office.

"Father MacKenzie," said Father Lewis, "The Bishop is not in a very good mood today, so I would take it with caution."

Father Bill replied, "Thank you, Father."

The office door opened into a rather large and ornate room with red wallpaper, brown shag carpeting, and with a large desk in the center behind which sat the Most Reverend Joseph Sullivan, Bishop of Evart. Bishop Sullivan is a man in his mid fifties, slightly overweight, graying hair, and standing he would be about 5 foot 6 inches tall. The good Bishop wears wire-rimmed glasses.

Bishop Sullivan stood up and said, "Welcome, Father MacKenzie."

Father Bill proceeded with the customary protocol of kissing the Bishop's Episcopal ring, a sign of his respect for his Bishop. He was then invited to sit for this visit.

Bishop Sullivan then decided to indulge in one of his vices, that of smoking the worst of cigars, they couldn't have been priced at more than 25 for a dollar. The aroma thus produced would be memorable as it could cause curling of eyelashes. Bishop Sullivan then began to fumble for some papers that were on his desk. Finally, he located the ones that he had been seeking.

Bishop Sullivan looked straight at Father Bill and said, "Let's cut through the crap and get right down to the meat of the subject at hand, OK Father?"

Father Bill took a deep breath, and said, "Yes, your Eminence."

"Eminence?", retorted the Bishop, "I said that we would cut through the crap, didn't I? Father MacKenzie, I have been reviewing your seminary file, and frankly, I am surprised that you made it all the way through your training."

This exchange with Bishop Sullivan has made Bill quite uneasy about his present situation, as the predicted bad mood was, indeed, true.

Father Bill's mind was now asking himself questions again: "What is he going to say next? Does he know about every prank that was gotten into at the school?" Father Bill's train of thought was broken by Bishop Sullivan.

"May I continue, Father MacKenzie? It says here in your seminary file, that you are a generally cut up, clown type priest. Your counselors say that it will be unlikely that you will ever be a success in a ministry of any kind. They even recommended that I delay your ordination pending an improvement in your demonstrable abilities, and in your attitude."

Bishop Sullivan paused for a few moments to generate a sizeable amount of freshly foul cigar smoke in Father Bill's direction. Bishop Sullivan then stood up and walked to the window. He could see the school kids from the parish school at their recess break.

"Father MacKenzie," the Bishop began again, "I intentionally ignored this report from the seminary. I did so because I felt that all of us deserve a chance, slim though it may be, and so, Father, after prayerful thought and meditation, I have decided to send you to a parish in the northern region of our diocese. This parish has a priest in residence at this time. He is Father Joe Williams. He is getting near retirement age and he has seen little in the way of success himself. I am praying that the two of you can help each other in the area of self improvement."

"Father MacKenzie, this assignment is for two years," the Bishop added.

Father Bill was stunned with this announcement, and began to speak, with a squeak in his voice, he said, "What parish will I be serving?"

Bishop Sullivan continued, "You are being assigned to St. Jerome parish in Antrim Junction. Joe Williams is a good man, but he lacks the abilities that are necessary to manage a big city parish. You, however, do not lack abilities when it comes to setting fire to the stools in the men's room, greasing those same toilet seats, and, here is the best one, you put a pig into the rector's car."

A surprised Father Bill began to squeak another stunned response, "You know about all of that student prank stuff at our school? I thought that that sort of thing was just between us students."

Bishop Sullivan began again, "On the contrary, Father MacKenzie, the rector at the school included all of your varied escapades in your personal file. It seems that you were an occupant of various lists that he maintains at the school. You didn't see eye to eye with him, did you?"

Father Bill began again, "I guess that I never really grew up completely, Father. I am still a boy at heart and I always enjoy a laugh. The rector of the school is a stuffed shirt, old hard liner from way back. He never smiles or ever seems to enjoy himself."

"Well, Father MacKenzie," the Bishop continued, "I hope that you will see eye to eye with the evil and the good that are present in Antrim Junction. The evil elements in that town include prostitution, many forms of gambling, drugs, and a rampant numbers racket. These are the everyday things that affect people in Antrim Junction. These evils are a part of Father Joe's failure to be a success in his ministry. I will call Father Joe and tell him to expect you in a few days. Are there any questions, Father?"

"No, I don't think so," said Father Bill, "It won't take me very long to get ready to move. Please tell Father Joe that I will be there on Thursday."

"OK" said Bishop Sullivan, "It's a deal."

During the walk back to the ante room entry, Father Lewis asked, "Are you OK, Father?"

Bill paused for a moment, and said, "I think so, the good Bishop seemed as though he wanted to stick it to me."

Father Lewis smiled, and said, "Well, Bishop Sullivan has been in a humanitarian mood these last few months. He is trying to shape up the priesthood in this diocese. Among those are priests like you, who seem to be a legend in their own minds, to whom he is giving challenging assignments as an attempt to shape their priesthoods in a positive way. It is his hope that you will come out of this assignment ready to have a pastorate of your own, and to be able to handle any and all things that are thrown at you in the future." Father Lewis escorted Father Bill back to the entry door.

Bill said, "Thank you, Father, I hope that Bishop Sullivan will see that positive result that he is seeking."

Father Lewis just smiled as he closed the door.

On the return trip to the seminary, Father Bill's mind was a jumble of questions: "Was Antrim Junction a hell hole? Were there prostitutes on every corner? Were there gambling opportunities at every turn of the road? Just what was there?"

Before Bill realized it, his trip back to the seminary was over. He had arrived at the dormitory that had been his home for the last five years. It seemed that the rehashing of the events of the morning through his mind had caused the trip back to the dorm to be a short one.

It was a well known fact that Bill would begin a rational and systematic packing of his belongings, and then, suddenly he would dump the remaining things into a big box and declare, "There, I'm done with that job."

*Father William MacKenzie*

# Chapter 2

## "Ian MacGregor"

Across the Atlantic Ocean, in the small mining town of Irvine, North Ayshire, in western Scotland, Ian MacGregor is just arriving home from school. Ian is a lad of five foot four, slender, and athletically built. He has blond hair and bright, blue eyes. He plays sports often including American football. Ian also loves Greco-Roman wrestling and he is a competitive swimmer.

It is a gray and overcast day in early March. There is a lot of rainfall on the British Isles today, as most days do not go by without some rain. Ian is just beginning his math homework, which is only part of an evening's toil.

While Ian is busy with his math homework, his close friends are at the school athletic field playing a game of American football. Ian had to skip the session as he had a lot of homework mostly math and an important essay which was due soon. Ian was feeling that, at last, he was making headway on his assignment, when suddenly, Ian's father, Andrew broke into his math world with a stunning announcement.

"Ian," Andrew shouted, "Gather your things together! Ian, didn't you hear me?" Andrew yelled again at the top of his voice.

"Ian, we are going to America!"

Ian slid back in his chair, puzzled, not knowing what to think. He remained quiet for a little while longer, thinking : "What could this be?"

Ian finally spoke to this father, "What is going on here? Why are you yelling so loud?"

Andrew sat down across from Ian and said, "We are going to America, as I have secured a wonderful chance to get along better in the world, and to get away from all of these strikes. I know that you are affected by these strikes, even though you are in school and have much lesson work to do. I know, because you haven't had your favorite donuts lately. The makings for the donuts are brought into our town on the trains from London. And, if Angus canna get the flours and other makings, he canna make your favorite treats."

Ian seemed to be a bit wary of the situation.

Ian said, "Father, why would we want to just pick up and leave our beloved fatherland to go to America. We would lose track of our friends, your buddies, and life long pals. You would miss out on the daily news gathering at the pub after work, and all the rest of the regular things that you do."

Andrew began again, "Ian, don't you remember, the strikes have made us the poorest that we have ever been and we canna go on doon the same stuff everyday. We are out of it. I have secured a chance for us to go to America and to put all of this behind us forever."

Ian paused, looked around the room and then began, "Father, this is our homeland, the land of our fathers, the fathers who fought for our pride and our heritage. Many hundreds of our ancestors died for what we have now. We enjoy a proud homeland. Sure, the strikes are deep this time, and we have little to eat, but we are still together, the three of us, and, God willing, we will make it!"

"Enough, enough!" yelled Andrew at his youngest son. "We are leaving in just two days, and you and Eric must get ready, and mind you, we are limited as to what we can take with us. So, look through your things, and take your clothing, school gear, and what ever else you can fit into three suitcases each!" Andrew continued, "That is exactly final, am I understood, Ian?"

"Aye, sir." Ian managed to say.

The whole event with his father came as a shock to Ian. The math assignment suddenly became moot. Ian's attention turned to his friends. He decided to go over to the school athletic field to see them.

As Ian approached the athletic field, he saw his best friend, Kevin MacLeod, leading his team to a small victory over their opponent. This was a game of American football. Kevin looked up and saw his friend standing there. Kevin knew at once that something was wrong.

"What's up?" Kevin asked.

"Well," Ian began, "I have some news that will surprise you." Ian hesitated to continue.

"What is it, Ian?" Kevin asked.

Ian said, "Well, my father came home in a strange mood just an hour ago, and he said that we were going to America forever. He has had it with all the strikes around here and of being poor all the time. I have just two days to pack my three suitcases, which is all that I can take away from here."

Kevin thought for a moment, and then began a defense for the fatherland. He said, "Isn't there anything that can be done? Can't your father realize that our futures are at stake with a move like this? He can't be serious."

Ian now feels that he has to be more firm with Kevin, and began again, "Well, Kevin, he was yelling at the end of our conversation, and basically, his decision is final. I don't know how we are traveling to the United States, or where. I only know that he has had it here and that he wants out desperately. I can't oppose him. He wants something better, and who could fault him for that? He lost our mum to illness a year ago, and since she died, he hasn't been the same proud father that we were used to for so many, many years."

Kevin grimaced, and said, "Ian, I will miss you forever. You are my best friend, and without you here, I won't be able to get through school. You always bail me out when I'm in trouble or if I need help with an essay. How will I be able to see you? Will I be able to talk to you on the phone?"

Ian was not wanting to come to total attention on Kevin's questions.

Ian said, "Kevin, we can write letters to each other, and maybe a phone call or two later on, we have to get settled, get working, and get back into school. I'll probably fall behind in my school work, and most likely, the American schools are on different schedules and have different courses to teach us."

Kevin stood up and hugged his pal, and said, "You won't ever forget me, will you, Ian? We were almost like one person here. You will always have that special place in my heart! Love you!"

Ian turned, and slowly left the field, a tear in his eye. His friend, Kevin who had always been in his life would no longer be there. How could he get along without him?

*Ian MacGregor*

## Chapter 3

# "Father Bill Comes To Antrim Junction"

Today is Thursday and Father Bill is on his way to his first assignment as a parish priest. He is driving his royally beat up Volkswagen Bug. He is getting close to his new home, Antrim Junction. Noticeable along the way are numerous automobile junk yards, advertising used auto parts. Also coming into view is the town water tower, bright white with green lettering: ANTRIM JUNCTION.

To Bill, this little town seems to be peaceful enough. A sign up ahead advises the location of the City Limits. This large ornate sign also had other information on it. There are public clubs meeting here like the Rotary, the Lions Club and youth soccer and wrestling clubs.

Within seconds of passing the City Limit sign, cop lights can be seen in Bill's rear view mirror. Bill is being pulled over. Father Bill watches the scene develop for this traffic stop. He watches in his mirror to see a very rotund woman dressed as a cop waddle up to his window.

"Do you know why I stopped you, sir?" addressed the cop to Bill.

"No, officer, I don't" Bill managed to say, as he observed that this cop's name is Vickie.

"Well, sir, you were driving 2 miles per hour over the speed limit. You must receive a ticket. Just what are you doing in Antrim Junction?" questioned Vickie.

Father Bill began, "I am the new associate pastor at St. Jerome parish, and I will be assisting Father Joe with the work at the parish."

Vickie screeched, "Oh, no, another stinking priest, we don't like priests here!"

While this exchange was under way with Vickie, Bill noticed that a black limo passed their location heading toward the business district. It seemed to Bill that the appearance of such a car was odd in this rural area.

Father Bill started again, "My assignment is for two years, and I hope that we will learn to work together here. I want to be a part of this community and live here in peace."

"You will have to see our beloved Judge Abner Stewart to resolve this serious infraction." stated Vickie quite firmly.

Bill began again, "May I inquire as to where the posted speed limit is to be seen for this stretch of road that I have allegedly violated?"

Vickie was a bit perturbed by this question, and said, "On the big sign at the City Limit where all the clubs are listed. There is a speed limit posted, 35 miles per hour, and you, sir, were going 37 miles per hour, a definite infraction!"

Vickie handed the ticket to Bill and said, "Good day to you sir!"

Bill now felt that he had been suckered by a speed trap on his first day in town. He turned his car around and drove back to the sign location. He looked over the sign and discovered that the 35 mile per hour notice was comparitively small when checked next to the club notices. Bill was now sure that a person would have to have rabbit vision in order to notice it on first viewing.

Father Bill decided that he should move on to better things, and set about to locate St. Jerome's church. While driving about town, he noticed several things that appeared to be odd. There were none of the ladies of the evening visible as Bishop Sullivan had alluded, however, there were several smaller adult males walking about carrying small paper bags. These persons were probably the number couriers. Bill was surprised that they seemed a bit overt about their presence and their mission. Here in Michigan, the numbers racket uses the numbers picked by the Michigan State Lottery, however, the local racketeers pay $100 cash more for each winning bet of four digit numbers, thus siphoning lottery dollars away for crime. The couriers were going about their routes unfettered.

As Bill continued his search, he passed the US Post Office. He noticed that the same black limo that had passed his speeding ticket scene was parked in front. It still seemed odd that there would be such a car in Antrim Junction.

Inside the post office, the local king pin of the numbers racket was attempting to retrieve his box mail. After he had opened his box and had removed the contents, he decided that the mail that he had been expecting was not present. He then began to beat on the rows of mail boxes with his cane. A voice was heard from behind the rack in the mail sorting area. "That is all the mail that is in here for you today, Mr. Hardwicke!"

Father Bill is keeping his eye out for the church steeple, the most common way of finding the local parish. He drove a little farther north on Main Street when he noticed the church steeple off to his right. He turned right on the next street and drove east to Roscommon Street, then turning right he was now right in front of an older red brick church building outlined in white trim. The sign in front of the church reads: Masses-Saturday Vigil 5PM, Sunday 10AM and 5PM, daily Masses 8:30AM and confessions were Saturday 10AM to 11AM.

The layout seemed to be quite normal, an older church building, along side of which is a modest rectory, with a two car attached garage. There are lots of shade trees around the site and behind the church is the school. Bill was now recalling another item on the City Limit sign. Antrim Junction is also the home of a small college called Montrose University.

Father Bill pulled into the driveway of the St. Jerome parish rectory, parked his car, got out, and went to the front door. Here, he discovered that this rectory is some sort of a fortress. Surveillance cameras are pointed at the entry walk and an intercom is in place at the door, adjacent to the door bell button. Bill rang the bell.

As Father Bill waited for the door to answer, he noticed that the cameras were moving to get a good look at him. Presently, a voice is heard on the intercom. "Who is it?" an old voice said.

"It's Father Bill MacKenzie, I am your new assistant." said Bill.

Suddenly the door flew open and Bill was yanked inside in an unceremonious manner. The door was slammed shut and locked behind him.

There, in front of Father Bill, is standing a little man, dressed in priestly attire, who must be Father Joe.

"Father Joe?" asked Bill.

Father Joe began his introduction, "Father Bill, I am so glad that you have arrived here in one piece. This is a bad town, with lots of vices, evil, and of course, governmental corruption. Bishop Sullivan called and told me that you would be here to assist me. I was quite surprised at the turn of events, but pleased, nonetheless. This town has many Scottish people living here. Montrose University here has many Scots on staff, and it is a wonderful breath of fresh air among this area's small colleges."

Father Bill began, "Well, Father Joe, I am pleased to meet you, and I look forward to being a member of the staff here. I don't know much about the town yet, but I have met Vickie, who gave me a speeding ticket about 47 inches north of the City limit sign."

Father Joe continued, "Vickie hassles everyone who enters town, so she can see who they are, and size them up. She is attached to the evil elements in town. Mr. Bud Hardwicke is the king pin of the local organized crime, and you will, undoubtedly meet him very soon. Bud hates priests, and he will want to tell you personally what your limits will be. You will find that all of these people who run things here seem to be attached to each other at the hips."

"A short inventory of these guys will reveal that Bud Hardwicke runs the evil in town. His brother, Dudley Hardwicke is the Chief of Police. Vickie is Bud's niece. Judge Abner Stewart is not related. However, his strings are connected to Bud. Our Mayor is Richard Leslie, a leader who has no clue as to what is going on. He is small in stature, always around, and he does as Bud directs. And, then there are the two stars of our local battle of the outrageous. That being Madame Blimpneflah and Henry Horton, who owns the Horton Phone Company. Madame is independently wealthy and is our local phone freak. Henry hassles Madame almost daily, asking her to make less calls on her ten lines so that other subscribers can have a chance of getting a dial tone." Father Joe stated these items matter of factly.

Father Bill began again, "I am now getting the picture to which the good Bishop was alluding. He seemed to relate to me that this town is a hell hole and that it has no redeeming value. I have only seen Vickie so far, and she could be a John Candy character in drag."

Father Joe replied, "You can make light of her all you want, but she is bad news. She can create instant havoc if she chooses and all of her cohorts will oblige her wishes."

Bill was seeing that he needed to start over, and said, "Father Joe, lets visit tomorrow about the work that we will do together, the break will allow me some time to get settled in my room. Sound like a deal?"

Joe replied, "Yes, of course, Father. Let me show you to your room, and, after you are settled, you can explore the site."

Bill began by carrying in his suitcases, and of course, the large box into which his final packing effort was stuffed. When all the unpacking was accomplished, Bill sat down in his room and looked out the window. He could see the kids playing in the baseball area. This view reminded Bill that the future rests in the kids. This impression would soon come home to him in great gushes.

*Vickie Hardwicke*

## Chapter 4
# "Ian Comes To The US"

Ian has left Scotland behind. After many hours in the air in a jumbo jetliner flying toward his new home in Antrim Junction, Michigan, Ian is now beginning to relax a little as he watches endless waves in the sea far, far below. At this altitude, it is quite difficult to make out much in the ocean.

Andrew MacGregor senses that his youngest son is quite troubled. Andrew said, "Ian, I know that this is all quite a shock to you. You have had to leave your best friend behind, and head to a country of which you have little knowledge. It is my prayer that the three of us will have a better life. Sometime soon, maybe Kevin can visit us in Antrim Junction."

Ian began to speak, "Father, I loved my Scottish homeland with all of my heart, and I will mourn for it for a time. I will miss Kevin always. He has been a very important part of my life. Missing him is like a trauma to my sense of well being. And, Father, don't forget there will be new friends in Michigan, and there will be a whole new lifestyle living on a college campus, and of going to school at St. Jerome's High School. New things will lighten up on the pressure that I feel right now. Sorry, Father, I canna share in your happiness right now, but soon."

When Ian had finished speaking, he turned to look out the window some more.

Eric is a solidly built Scottish lad with a deep voice. He began to speak to his father, "Father, I won't miss Scotland, and all of the turmoil, agitation, and mostly the strife from all of the strikes. Ian, on the other hand, is mourning the loss of his homeland, and he regrets being here with us. Ian would have been the apple of your father's eye had he known Ian. He is a faithful person when it comes to heritage. He loves Scotland, his kilts, bagpipes, and all the like."

Andrew grimaced, and said, "I know, it pains me to see him so sad. He did say that he will find some new friends in Michigan, and that school will occupy his time."

The flight continued for a few more hours before Ian could see land appearing below, but even then, they did not put down. The plane, instead, continued on for about three more hours, and then an announcement was heard.

"Folks, this is Captain Gould, your pilot, and along with my crew, we are welcoming you to Detroit, Michigan, as we are approaching Detroit/Wayne County Metropolitan Airport in the United States, please be prepared to go through customs upon deplaning here. Have your passports ready."

Ian began to stir around in his seat in anticipation of the arrival in Michigan. The airport looks to be of the huge variety. It is composed of several different terminals. As the pilot taxied the plane up to the staging area, Ian could see that a large number of people were required to receive his plane here in Detroit. Finally, the plane came to a stop. The ground crew began the process of bringing in the baggage trucks to take the checked luggage to the claim area. Presently, the flight attendants indicated that their passengers could retrieve their carry-on luggage that had been stowed in the overhead compartments.

Andrew, Ian, and Eric gathered up their carry-on things. They are now discovering that their legs are crampy as they had been seated for a long time since leaving the United Kingdom. All of the passengers dutifully fell into line and moved toward the exit hatch. Ian was aware that a new world awaited him in the terminal and beyond. This is his new home, Michigan in the United States of America.

Andrew said, "Let's get something to eat before the next flight. Ian, we have just one more short flight to go, and then we will have to drive up to Antrim Junction from Grand Rapids."

Ian managed a small smile, as he felt that this break was needed for all three of them. Ian could now see the local concourse area from their encounter with the US customs service. He could see various food establishments that were offering fast food. Food on the run? This sort of food must be needed here in the airport for people who are traveling and who have very little time between planes.

Andrew looked around, and said, "Let's try Burger King!"

Andrew's voice was not as strong as it usually is, so Ian felt that his father was unsure of just what Burger King is.

Inside the restaurant, the three of them noticed that people were lined up to place their orders, and then they were to move on to a self-serve pop station to fill their own drink cups, and to yet another place to claim their order, as no server would be bringing their order to their table. In Scotland, the only time that the MacGregors would eat out was at a formal sort of eatery where there were servers, menus, and good service.

It was good to have something to eat, but Ian could have waited for what some of the local people called real food. He was preoccupied with what was outside, only to remember that they would soon board another plane, and head to northern lower Michigan. Another twenty minutes went by and then it was time to look for the boarding location for the next flight. They left Burger King. The plane at the next dock was quite a bit smaller than the plane that had carried the MacGregors here from Scotland. In fact, this little plane was a propeller plane, it had two engines, and it would seat about 40 passengers and a crew of three.

To top off everything, they had to walk out on the tarmac to board the plane, as it was too short to match up to the regular jet dock. During the walk out to the plane, Ian noticed that it was painted red and that it was labeled Northwest Airlink. When all was ready, the pilots began the start up procedure, and soon the plane moved away from the boarding area, taxied a short time, and was airborne in a few minutes, heading northwest from the Detroit Airport. The crew announced that the trip would take about two hours.

This leg of the trip was quite a bit more interesting. They were flying much lower than the flight from the UK. Ian could see lots of things about Michigan as they went on. The most striking feature that Ian noticed was that there were countless lakes and ponds visible. Many streams could also be seen. This leg of the trip ended all too soon, as the small plane was beginning to descend for a landing at the Gerald R. Ford International Airport near Grand Rapids.

Ian asked his father, "Where do we go from here?"

Andrew paused to answer his son, "There is a car here for us to use, and I have the keys. This car is a red one, labeled "Montrose University"." Soon, they located the car, which was indeed ready for them. Maps and directions were found on the drivers seat. The notes found on the seat indicated that the trip to Antrim Junction would take about two and one half hours. They hadn't realized it yet, but these Americans drive on the other side of the road from the drivers at home. Andrew would have to adjust to this.

# Chapter 5

## "Arrival"

Father Bill had just entered the rectory after a midday walk about Antrim Junction. He noticed that Father Joe was seated at the dining room table, working on his daily crossword puzzle.

Joe looked up, and said, "Well, Father, what have you discovered about the Junction today?"

"Well," Bill began, "I, needless to say, have been questioned by Vickie again. She seems to think that I am here on some clandestine mission cooked up by Bishop Sullivan, for whom she has a sizeable mistrust."

Joe interrupted Bill's train of thought, "It might interest you to know that Madame called me this morning. The old bat hasn't bothered to call here in many weeks, but, She chose to call today to inform me that there is a new priest in town and that he could not be trusted. It seems that this priest, in the opinion of Madame, has been placed here at the behest of Bishop Sullivan, with the intention of bringing Antrim Junction to its literal knees."

"Wow," exclaimed Father Bill, "Madame has had the rumor mill in high gear and on overtime right from the start. I will endeavor to bring about ministry wherever opportunity presents itself."

"Bill," Joe Williams began in a more stern voice, "I would not do anything to upset the applecart just yet. You will need to try to fit in here, and to be a part of the St. Jerome's family. The criminal elements present here have been in town a long time and they control most of what goes on here. If we go about our everyday lives, they won't bother us."

Bill said, "But Father Joe, these things that the crime people do are morally wrong, create social decay, and engender vices in our young people. Father, I view the young people as our cherished source of the future, and thus they need to be nurtured and trained to be worthy of being that future. It will be difficult for me to just sit back and let them harm our children."

"I know, I know," Joe began again, "I have lived here in this rectory for twenty years and I have had little success among the people here. No notoriety and no thanks for a job done, or anything of the kind. I baptize their children, I do their weddings, and bury their dead, and sometimes I even hear their confessions. It is not the kind of priesthood that I had dreamed about while I was being trained. I live a sheltered life here. I am seen only on the weekends, during Mass, and harassed on schedule in order to keep me in line."

Bill was feeling a lack of compassion for Joe Williams, who, as Bishop Sullivan had related, has not been a successful priest in his own right.

Bill said, "Father, I promise you that I will not intentionally embarrass you here, but I also promise you that I will be a priest in every sense of the word."

Father Joe was surprised at Bill's reaction, and said, "Father Bill, I think it is best that we start slowly here and introduce you to the parish this Saturday night at the vigil Mass. I will concelebrate this Mass with you and we will be a big hit. Further, I will schedule a get acquainted event for after the Mass, so the parishioners can meet you personally."

Bill was a bit startled by Father Joe's sudden burst of authority.

Bill said, "Yes, sir, Father, I think that is a perfect idea and I will prepare my charisma for it."

Since spring was lingering on in Antrim Junction, the days were a bit cool and the nights were cold. Bill had additional adjustments to make. It seems that Father Joe is expecting a productive curate in him and he must prepare himself to live up to that expectation. Bill went on another walk after leaving Joe to his puzzle. He decided to walk up to the high school to check things out and he was justly proud of the idea to do so. The high school was located on a large land parcel behind the church. The school was created to accommodate up to 400 students in grades 9 through 12. The trip to the school took about 5 minutes, during which, Bill noticed that there was a baseball diamond and a football field complete with bleachers that could seat a few hundred fans. This seemed to please Bill, as he believes in healthy athletic efforts daily.

Upon entry to the school, a voice was heard, "May I help you sir?"

Bill turned around, he could see that the voice came from a young woman, who was probably a senior who works part-time in the school office.

"Oh, I'm sorry, Father, I didn't realize that you were a priest. From behind, I couldn't tell, I am so sorry."

Bill interrupted, "I am Father Bill MacKenzie, the new associate pastor here at St. Jerome's, and I am exploring the campus."

The young woman began again, "Father, I am Elise Leslie, my folks are longtime residents at the Junction, and my uncle is mayor here. I'm a senior this year, and I will graduate in just a few months."

Father Bill smiled, and said, "Well, Elise, I'm pleased to meet you, and I hope to meet lots of new folks this Saturday night, as I will share Mass with Father Joe. My mission today is to familiarize myself with the layout of the buildings, and to meet some of the people who run them."

Elise added, "Father, you know, I'm sure, that this is not the greatest of towns, but there are a lot of great people here, people who need a fresh guy like you to pooch up their spirits and help them set new goals for themselves. Have you met Vickie yet?"

Bill quipped, "Yes, just inches north of the City Limit sign, and I was awarded a ticket for going two miles per hour over the speed limit."

Elise smiled and added, "Judge Stewart is a puppet of the political machine here, and he will be prompted to stick it to you. They are all hooked together in some way and they manage to run most things here."

Father Bill decided, upon digesting the comments that were made by Elise, that there is, indeed, some kind of under current here running things. Further, Bill reasoned that he would have to, at some point, find a way to inject himself into one of these vice arteries in order to water down their effectiveness.

Meanwhile, Andrew MacGregor and his family are traveling north through the Michigan countryside. Ian was noticing that there is plenty of farming going on in this area and some fields were already being prepared for the upcoming planting. Some farms were devoted to dairy, while others grew the feed for the dairy farms.

Grand Rapids has a lot of business activity going on, many groupings of stores, which Ian would learn to call malls or shopping centers. There were a lot of those places called "Burger King" like Ian first sampled at the Detroit Airport. It seems that, here

*Elise Leslie*

in Michigan, life is fast paced and this leaves little time for family interaction at the dinner table, which, to Ian, seemed important lately.

Fast food wasn't the only thing that affected the pace of life. There was the radio in the car on which Ian hears a new form of communication that the host of which called music. Ian knew that his father would not agree that it was anything of the sort. The music on the radio was presented at a past pace and the announcer informed the listener that this was the first of ten in a row. The guy never said the time of day, nor the weather forecast, and didn't say any news at all.

Andrew MacGregor began to speak, "Ian, have you noticed that this is a nice place to live? It seems that everyone knows what they should be doing, and are in the process of getting it accomplished. Drivers on the road seem to be in a hurry to get where they are going, and also seem to have a targeted time for their arrival.

Ian broke his silence, "Father, how much farther do we have to go? This ride is scary, as we are experiencing your learning to drive on American roads, quite different from home."

Ian continued, "I can see that this place has a lot of promise for our future. Lots of things are under way here. I have seen a lot of farming, building, road construction, and lots of smiling faces."

Andrew noticed the first positive feelings coming from Ian with his remarks. He said, "I think that we have about another half hour or so to go before we get there. There are many signs along the way that mention Antrim Junction.

They passed an IGA grocery store, and then the road went into a series of S-curves. Then, suddenly straight ahead there was the stark white water tower with bright green lettering: "Antrim Junction" written on it. Also, quite quickly, there came into view an ornate

City Limit sign. Ian could see the names of the local clubs clearly posted and he also noticed that the speed limit was posted.

"Father, slow down," said Ian, "The speed limit is posted 35 MPH."

Andrew reacted at once and slowed down. This quick reduction in speed caused Vickie to take notice of the car, a local one, the caretaker's car to be specific, with unknown people on board. This would, in Vickie's opinion, need checking out.

Andrew was maintaining about 30 MPH so as to not deserve the attention of the constabulary. Vickie pulled out and began to follow the red college car. Andrew caused the car to slow some more, as he was unsure of where he was going. He was confident that the police that had been following him would know, so he pulled over and so did Vickie.

Vickie waddled up to the driver's window of the college car, and she said, "Can I help you find something here in Antrim Junction? You know, you are driving a car that belongs to Montrose University, here in town, and I am unaware of who you are, and why you should have this car."

Andrew was aware that Vickie had scoped out his family as she approached the car. He felt a little uneasy with this situation. Andrew spoke to Vickie, "I am Andrew MacGregor. These two fellows are my sons. I'm the new groundskeeper at the college, and we are freshly arrived from Scotland. The college folks left this car for us to use while driving here from the Ford Airport in Grand Rapids. They left directions to get to Antrim Junction. The only problem that I'm having is finding the precise location of the campus."

Vickie seemed a little miffed that she had not uncovered some covert operation and she said, "Continue north on the main drag here until you get to Roscommon Avenue. Turn right and enter the campus service drive, turn left and go north for two blocks, the caretaker's house is on the right, building 14."

Andrew was grateful for Vickie's help, and said, "Thanks officer, have a wonderful day."

Vickie replied, "Hurrumpfh."

# Chapter 6
# *"Ian Checks out Antrim Junction"*

Tomorrow will be Saturday, and Ian felt that it was time to look up St. Jerome's Catholic Church. Ian wanted to get settled in and there seemed to be no better way to do that than to go to Mass, where he can meet some people. The church was about a half mile walk south on the service drive from the caretaker's house. The walk, as always, was fine with him.

The church steeple was straight ahead. Ian knew that this would be his spiritual home from now on. Inside, it looked like an old church with lots of ornate furnishings throughout. The parish candle was hung aloft on the left side of the sanctuary, its red candle glow symbolized the vibrant life in the spirit of its members. Ian could sense the homey feel of this place. Ian sat down and was soaking up the ambiance of this rural home-style room when he heard a noise behind him. He was slightly surprised. Ian turned around to see a young priest coming in through the main door.

The priest waked up to Ian, and said, "Hi, I am Father Bill MacKenzie, the curate here. I am glad to see you."

Ian introduced himself, "Hello, I am Ian MacGregor, a new arrival at the college. My father is the new caretaker. We have just arrived here from Scotland. I will be starting to attend St. Jerome's

High School this coming Monday. You, Father, are the first person that I have met here since meeting Vickie."

Father Bill managed a small smirk, and said, "Yes, it seems that she does not miss a chance to size up all people who cross into the City at the limit sign. I got a speeding ticket just inches north of the sign only yesterday, when I also got into Antrim Junction for my first day at St. Jerome's."

Father Bill continued, "There is a special Mass tomorrow night at 5PM at which I will be introduced to the people of St. Jerome's, it will also be a good time to introduce you and your family. The caretaker at the college is a very important person to us. He takes care of the land and building exteriors, and keeps that facility a gleaming treasure in our community."

Ian was a bit surprised at hearing this flowery description from Father Bill, who, himself, has only been in Antrim Junction just as many hours as Ian.

Ian said, "Father Bill, I hope that we can be friends. I will need to know people here. I know nothing about this place, let alone much about the US. It will be a learning experience every minute."

The two of them chatted for a few more minutes, and then they went their separate ways. Bill resumed the preparations for the Mass and Ian continued his walk about town.

Ian found that the business area was just a few blocks from St. Jerome's church. His inspection of the main blocks revealed an ice cream store, where Mooney's ice cream cones could be purchased, hand packed. A drug store called Rite Aid, and a collection of petrol filling stations were noted. He was amused that the Americans call petrol "gasoline" or "gas". Further, the various petrol stations had their prices high up on placards where the price for regular was tooted for all to see.

Continuing on, Ian observed several groups of teens gathered in front of what they called a party store. These teens were of similar age as Ian. He felt that he would surely see them Monday at school. None of the kids even showed the slightest notion that they knew that he was there.

Walking on, Ian began to feel strange about some of the adults that were out and about in the city as he was walking north on Main Street. There were little men standing on the corners holding small paper bags. These bags were well traveled, as they were wrinkled from being opened and closed often. These men seemed to want to be secretive about their mission, all of which eluded Ian at the moment.

Ian decided to walk east at the next street, so that his walk would return him to the southward path that he took to find the church. This was Elm Street. It had many small homes, except that, right in the middle of the block, on the south side of the street, there stood a three story house that had strange rounded gables. This huge, gaudy, yellow house gave forth a sense of the macabre. Ian walked closer to the mailbox, so that he could read the name on it. The name was: "Madame Blimpneflah". What a strange name, he thought. Who could this be? An ugly yellow house with a yellow picket fence, and a yellow mailbox to match, with a strange name on it.

Ian was not aware of Madame's surveillance, but she was, indeed, watching him intently as he walked past her house. Madame, being the foremost authority in Antrim Junction, would form an immediate impression of Ian, and it would be known all about town soon. For, you see, Madame is the town's phone freak, having ten lines installed into her house, and they are connected to several call director consoles, so as to be able to conduct her gossip mission most effectively.

Ian will experience the results of Madame's influence as the days and months pass. Ian paused one last time, turned, and looked back to check that he had actually seen that strange ugly house. As he did so, suddenly there was a quick closing of the curtain in a front room. He was now convinced that he had seen the house.

Ian continued his walk east on Elm Street. Up ahead, he saw a step ladder placed up to a stop sign. There was a small man on the ladder. It appeared that this fellow was polishing the stop sign.

Ian walked up and spoke to the man, "Hello there."

The man looked up, and was all smiles. He said, "Hi."

Ian began to introduce himself, "I am Ian MacGregor, and I am new to Antrim Junction. I have come here from Scotland with my father and older brother, Eric. My father is the new caretaker at the college, and we have taken up residence on the campus."

The sign polisher, now down on the ground, began to speak, "Hello, I am very pleased to meet you, Ian. I am Albert Leslie. I do menial jobs for the City. My brother is the mayor here. He thinks that I am retarded, and that I can only do little jobs, like polishing stop signs."

Ian replied, "I am pleased to know you. I do not know anything about this place, except, that I have met Father Bill MacKenzie, who is new to St. Jerome's parish. He has been in town the same length of time that we have. I am walking around to discover what I can about Antrim Junction. That's when I came across you, Albert."

Albert continued, "Ian, I am always pleased to meet someone new. There are lots of different people in the world, and the chance to meet them all is limited, but now I know one more of them. You, Ian, are a welcome addition to our community. I think that you will like this town. There are lots of Scots in residence here. Just look in the Horton Phone book and check just the Mac listings, there are lots of them."

A different sort of a look came over Albert's face, and he said,

"Ian, I must tell you of the bad things here. This town has a numbers racket that extends out into the county. This crime is operated by one Bud Hardwicke. Bud uses the Michigan Lottery to pick the numbers, he pays bigger prizes, and this helps him take lottery dollars away for crime."

"To make his web work, Bud has his niece Vickie patrol the City in a cop car, she pulls people over to see who they are. If these victims are someone, then she alerts Madame Blimpneflah, who coordinates the evasive action. In order to enforce anything, Bud has placed his brother Dudley in office as the Chief of Police. Daily, the couriers gather the money and the bet slips for the numbers, and transfer them to the black limo via Bud's chauffeur. As time goes on, you will learn to recognize these people. They are bad, and they run things in this town."

Ian was surprised to hear this stuff. He said, "Albert, how long has this been going on?"

Albert replied, "Bud and his boys have been working the numbers for a long time, probably about 15 years. He says he has molded this town to his liking, and he means to keep it like that and to force it to make lots of money in the process."

Ian said, "Albert, I hope that this do-dah will not interfere with going to school. I need to get a re-start in school. Classes here are different, and they will have to be matched up with what I have accomplished thus far in school at home."

Albert, now smiling, said, "Ian, if you go about your daily activities, they won't bother you, but if you try to interfere with them, they will fight back. I just thought that it was fair to let you know to watch for this stuff. I hope to see you around. I gotta finish this polishing job, and get up the street. See ya."

Ian was now at the service drive that led back to the north, and to his new home at Montrose University. Turning left, Ian was now headed back home, and to the task of getting unpacked and settled. After all, he would be in the throes of school work on Monday, along with the pressure of getting up to the pace of classes here. The whole prospect of going to school in the US was a completely unknown factor to him.

Andrew came into the caretaker's house just after Ian had entered. Andrew, in an excited voice, said, "Ian, I just love this place! It is more than I had dreamed that it could be. They have all of the right equipment to do the work here, and the dean, to whom I report, is quite a nice fellow. He is anxious that we will like it here and that we will stay here for a long time."

Ian was surprised to learn of his father's new found happiness. Ian said, "I have been walking about the town this afternoon, and I have met Father Bill MacKenzie, who is a newly ordained priest, and he has just arrived here the same day that we got here. He is serving as the new associate pastor at St. Jerome's. I have also located the local business area, the petrol filling stations, and a couple of groups of teenagers, who did not seem very friendly. Father Bill said that it would be good for us to go to the vigil Mass on Saturday so that we too can be introduced as new members of the community and I assured him that we would be there."

Andrew, still sporting a gleaming grin, said, "I am happy that you have made the first efforts at getting acquainted here. Ian, we will indeed be at the Mass, as I too, feel that it is important to be a part of the local family."

Ian began again, "But, father, as I was walking on

Elm Street, I saw a strange house, which has a definite strange feeling about it. And, there was a strange name on the mailbox, Madame Blimpneflah. Someone seemed to be spying on my as I walked past that house. And, when I turned around to look again, the curtain suddenly closed."

Andrew was amused with what Ian was saying, and then said, "Ian, I suppose every town has its strange people, and it would not be that uncommon. Let's be happy that we are here, and let Madame be to herself for now. Where has Eric gone?"

Ian replied, "I haven't seen Eric since early this morning. Maybe he is still exploring Antrim Junction. He's not excited about being here, although one cannot tell about him. He does not show much emotion. He's stuffy sometimes."

Andrew responded, "It will be OK, Eric will soften up, and he will find a job, and then decide on a future for himself here in the US. He gets free tuition at the college and he can get a viable degree there. One that will make him a success in America."

Ian left for his room and for the task of unpacking, a job which would be similar to the procedure used by Father Bill. Ian unpacked, first of all, his most prized clothing items, his kilts. The tartan pattern was precisely that of the MacGregors of years past, true to his grandfather's heritage, down to the last and smallest detail.

Ian then opened his stash of notes and addresses of friends, now thousands of miles away, to remember his friend, Kevin, and at the same time he was wondering what Kevin was doing today? In fact, Kevin was in a panic to learn the math that Ian had made so easy for him to learn.

The goings on in Scotland were not visible to Ian, but nevertheless, it is firmly in his heart as he pines for his fatherland. He knows that he must come to grips with the fact that he must make Antrim Junction his home and maybe a new fatherland.

Ian was curious to look in the local phonebook. He picked it up, and on the cover in big letters, it read, "Horton Phone Company,

Antrim Junction, Michigan". The volume was very plain, and had only about 105 pages with some of them yellow for advertising. His mission with this curiosity was to verify what Albert Leslie had told him about the large Scottish population here. To Ian's surprise, there were over a hundred Mac names, as well as common clans such as Cameron, Gordon, Leslie, Scott, and Kincaid.

Ian smiled, and thought, "This just may be OK after all."

*Madame Blimpneflah*

# Chapter 7

# *"The First Mass"*

Saturday afternoon was a very pleasant experience in Antrim Junction. High pressure had delivered a pristine clear blue sky. A slight warming trend was evident, as the afternoon high was to be 43 degrees. The birds seemed to be happy, sounding forth their distinctive songs, and the squirrels were scurrying about seeking their stashed food. Across the campus, Ian could hear the church bells tolling a call to Mass.

This impressed Ian, as the custom of calling to Mass seemed to be forgotten elsewhere. Ian spoke to his father, "It's time to head down to the church. Can you hear the bells? Wonderful, isn't it?"

Andrew was instantly pleased at what Ian was saying, as it seemed that Ian may be feeling a bit more at home here in Antrim Junction.

Andrew said, "Well, Ian, let's get about to go to the church. Is Eric around?"

Ian said, "Eric is in his room, shall I call out to him?"

"Yes," Andrew replied. "I want him to go with us. He won't be happy about it, but it's important this time."

Ian moved toward the bedroom area of the caretaker's house, and called out to Eric, "Eric, please come down. It's time to leave for Mass. Father wants you to go with us. Its important."

Eric snapped, "Go soak your head, Ian."

Andrew overheard Eric's treatment of Ian, and spoke, "Eric, you are to present yourself before me at once, without the slightest whimper about going to Mass. We have a lot to be thankful for, and thanking the Lord at Mass is most appropriate. We came to the US safely, and in good shape, and we have a fine new home."

Eric came into the parlor at once, and said, "Aye, sir, father, I am ready to go with you."

Andrew said, "That is more like it. Let's go. We are walking."

And so, the three MacGregors started their walk south toward St. Jerome's Catholic Church. During the walk, they met many others who were walking to church. This seemed to impress Ian, as the walking trip to church could enhance the family experience of it, making it more precious.

Inside the church, the MacGregors sat down in a pew about half way up the aisle. They looked around, and it appeared that about three hundred people were here. Ian was happy to see so many people who were obviously happy to be together.

Mass began and continued as Ian was used to it. At the time for the homily, Father Joe Williams came to the pulpit.

Father Joe began, "Welcome, welcome to a very special Mass of Joy. We have joy for we have a new associate pastor joining us here at St. Jerome's. You have seen him here with me during Mass. He is Father Bill MacKenzie, a recently ordained priest. He has been assigned here by our beloved Bishop Sullivan. It is my prayer that Father Bill will receive a warm welcome from all of you and that you will make him feel at home here. He is anxious to be part of a vibrant parish community, one where everyone knows everyone."

"Father Bill is a youngster when compared to an old fossil as myself. I am looking forward to his making the rectory more lively. Let us not wait another moment, may I present Father Bill!"

A round of applause began, as the people at Mass welcomed Father Bill to their parish. Bill felt a bit embarrassed as he began his address.

"Thank you for that wonderful welcome. I am here in my first assignment as a priest. I was ordained just last month at the Cathedral in Evart, Bishop Joseph Sullivan presiding. I thought that he was going to send me to a prominent parish in a big city at which I would experience lofty goals that I dreamed of during my training. However, the good Bishop, in his wisdom, has selected St. Jerome's as a good starting point, and now I know for sure that this is the right assignment for me."

Father Bill continued, "I trust that you will want to be active Catholic Christians in pursuit of heavenly happiness, as I am. Our goal is to arrive at that promised land together. Together, with you, this journey will be a pleasant one. I know, already, that there is much love in this parish for the Christ, and it feels like it, very, very much."

Another round of applause greeted Father Bill, much to his surprise. Bill felt a reddening coming over his face as he felt a little embarrassed.

Bill said in reply, "Thank you so much. I do, indeed feel at home here. Let me also ask that you extend your welcome to Mr. Andrew MacGregor and his sons Ian and Eric. They are newly arrived here from Scotland and they have taken up residence in the caretaker's house at the college. Ian will begin school on Monday at our own St. Jerome's High School. Please stand up, MacGregors, and let us welcome you too."

Andrew and Eric were surprised at this turn of events, but they stood up along with Ian and accepted the applause of another welcome. Andrew gave into a wide grin himself, and along with Father Bill, he felt at home here.

After Mass, many people stopped to chat with Andrew and his sons. They felt very welcomed indeed. Andrew was feeling good about the whole deal.

Andrew asked, "Ian, just how did Father Bill know all about us?"

Ian replied, "Well, during my first walk around town, I stopped in at the church where I met Father Bill. He was in the church working. I told him about our family, and how we had come to Antrim Junction from Scotland, and that we, too, were new arrivals here. He then asked me if we would be so kind as to come to this Mass, so we could share in the welcome, and that we could meet some of the locals at the reception, which we did."

Andrew said, "Its OK, Ian, I just wondered. We will fit in here nicely, I think."

Ian added, "Father, just look in the telephone book, and you can see all the Scottish names that are living here. I agree with you, Father, that we have to fit in here. It is our home now, like it or not, Eric?"

Eric snapped, "Whatever you say, Ian."

Andrew was not in a hurry to get back home, and so he slowed his pace so that he could take in the points of interest. The High School, the Grade School, the football field, the soccer field, and up ahead the college campus of Montrose University which was now his responsibility to take care of.

## Chapter 8

# "Bill Meets Bart"

Monday morning, after breakfast, Father Bill went to his office. He began to sort out some of his notes from the most recent classes that he had completed at the seminary. After about an hour or so, the telephone rang. It was quickly answered by someone. About a minute later, a young woman came to his office door to announce that the phone call was for him.

This turn of events took him by surprise. Bill picked up the phone, and said, "Hello, this is Father MacKenzie."

The caller began to speak, "Father, this is Madame Blimpneflah. You do not know me. I am calling to inform you that you have already overstepped your bounds as curate here in Antrim Junction. You said many pious things in your introduction. Things that the people here are not allowed to hope for. Do not think for a moment that you will always be received in the same manner as you were at the Mass on Saturday night."

Bill was a bit stunned, and said, "Madame, I assure you that I have all the latest training in priesthood and that I intend to bring my mission to fruition with whatever means it takes to give these people the gifts of the living Christ, and to help them to have Him in their everyday lives."

"More pious poppycock!" screamed Madame, "You sound like one of those radio preachers talking via taped delay. All talk sounds canned. There are established entities in Antrim Junction that will not ever abide in you having such freedom to minister. Father Joe has been held at bay for years, and you will be also, mark my words. Good day to you sir!"

The telephone line went dead.

Bill slid back in his chair. He was not wanting to believe what had just happened. Questions began racing through his mind: "What was the purpose of her call? Who are the entities? What could these people do to harm the parish?"

Presently, Father Joe came by the door to Bill's office. Joe noticed that Bill seemed to be in a dither, and said, "What's up. Bill?"

"Well," Bill began, "I just talked to Madame on the phone. I must say that I am stunned by the threatening tone of her call. She reported that the entities here in town have stifled you for years, and that I am next, and I will, in effect, see my ministry suppressed."

Father Joe, upon hearing this, came into Bill's office and sat down. He began to speak to Bill, "Bill, I am not surprised that she called you, after all, she is our phone freak, and she makes about two hundred calls a day. Also, I am not surprised at the tone of voice that she took with you. The entity that she mentioned is Bud Hardwicke. He runs the evil here. He has chosen to suppress St. Jerome's mission to its people ever since I came here. This effort of his has prevented me from having any success here as pastor. He is the king pin of the numbers racket. He has a prostitution effort, and he has sold drugs, all of which is regular business for him. The star effort is, of course, the numbers.

"Father Bill, it is time that you realize more clearly what the Bishop alluded to in his introduction of this assignment for you.

I am sure that he said the bit about my success here. You may try to overcome Bud's efforts, if you want, but I am too old to be of much help. Bud pulls all the governmental strings here in Antrim Junction, which is true to form for small town political machines."

"Vickie is the first line of notification. Anytime that she sees you ministering to someone, she will hassle you to the nth degree. Then up the chain of all the puppets, they all will know that you have surpassed the Hardwickes's plan for you, and then you will have to be punished. I suggest that you keep your car in the garage, with the garage door locked shut."

Father Bill was stunned at hearing this report from Joe, and he then decided to pursue the line with him.

"Father Joe, we can't let this Hardwicke fellow run our lives. He can't keep Jesus from our people. I will figure out how to bring this guy down. This town deserves to be free from these things."

Father Joe stood up, and said, "Father, you are welcome to try. I once had this same spirit that I am hearing from you but I was unable to bring the lofty goals to be. Bill, you are a fine young priest, but you need to learn about the wide variety of personalities that are found in a town like this. And remember your own heritage is Scottish, and I know that the Scot stubbornness is now driving your presentation. Bill, remember, you need to visit the high school each afternoon to see if counseling from you is needed."

Bill replied, "Oh, Father, I had not given the slightest of notions about my own heritage, I just think that what is wrong is wrong, and something should be done about it."

Father Joe managed a smile, and left Bill's office.

Bill slid back in his chair to think over the events of the morning. At this time, it seemed that the Hardwickes had won, and that was possibly why Madame had called him today. Bill sat in silence for a while, and then went to the dining room where Father Joe was waiting to have lunch.

After lunch, Bill was due to go over to the high school. At 1:00 he started his walk to the school. When he got into the main lobby, there was a disturbance in the main hall, just down from the principal's office. Bill found himself pushing his way through the small crowd of kids to find out what was going on. Much to his surprise, there was Ian MacGregor squaring off with a thug sort of fellow.

Ian looked up, and said, "Hello, Father Bill."

Bill stepped forward, and inserted himself between the two kids. He said, "Just what is going on here?"

The thug fellow said, "This new guy had to be told just who runs things here at St. Jerome's, and just where he fits in here. He is new and now he is informed."

"Just what is your name, sir?" asked Bill.

The young man replied, "Bart Hardwicke."

Bill is now beginning to figure things out. Here in Antrim Junction, the Hardwicke's rule over most folks who let them. Here in the high school was Bud's grandson, carrying out the old man's orders. Bill decided that the two of them must visit the principal's office for discipline.

Bill said, "You two report to the principal's office, and the rest of you get on to your classes. We are not going to tolerate bullying here at St. Jerome's."

Ian did not know how to react to the situation. He did as Father Bill had directed. Bart was reluctant to comply, but did. When the two of them got to the office, they were told to sit and wait for Father Bill to exit from his meeting with Mr. Kelley.

Once Father Bill left the principal's office, Ian was summoned in to see Mr. Kelley. He said, "What happened out there?"

Ian replied, "Bart felt that it was his place to inform me who runs things here. It is with assumed authority of his grandfather that he does this."

"How can you be sure that the Hardwickes are running things here?" asked the principal.

Ian began his answer, "I just have a feeling. He seems to be in tune with the likes of Vickie, whom we met just a few feet north of the city limit sign the day that we arrived here."

The principal, with a drawl, said, "Well, I want you to avoid Bart for now. Try to keep things under control. After all, your job here is to get educated."

Ian, feeling relieved, said, "Aye, sir."

Ian left Mr. Kelley's office and went on to his class.

Mr. Kelley went to the waiting room and said, "Bart, get to class."

Bart left immediately, and he was sporting a big grin on his face, as his place in things here got him off once again. Bart rushed past Father Bill in the hallway still showing his grin of triumph. Bill stood there amazed for a few moments. Shaking his head in disbelief, he thought that he should return to his own office.

As Bill was passing by the office, he heard Elise speak to him, "Father, would you come in here before you go?"

Father Bill went into the office again and went to where Elise was working.

"Hello, again," said Bill.

Elise said, "Father, please come into the conference room for a minute."

Once in the conference room, with the door closed, Elise said, "Father, it is unfortunate that you saw the exchange between Ian and Bart. Bart practically runs this school, he is backed up by Bud and his machine."

Father Bill began to speak, "Elise, I am surprised about the depth to which the Hardwickes control almost everything here in town. I was warned by Bishop Sullivan that the vices are the everyday thing things here. I came here with my eyes open, and to my surprise, most people cower to the Hardwickes. I have even been called by Madame, just this morning. I received a sort of a threat from her. I am determined, as Father Joe points out, being driven by my Scottish stubbornness to bring down the Hardwickes."

Elise managed a small smile, and said, "Father, you need to go easy in your efforts. I am not going to tell you not to try, just be safe."

Bill said, "Thanks you your concern. I don't know how to do it, but someone has to bring this guy down. It will require some thought. I am also concerned about Ian. He is new here, and I fear that he doesn't fully understand how the Hardwicke's efforts can drag down a whole town. Thanks, again."

Bill left for his office.

# Chapter 9
## "Bill Meets Bud Hardwicke"

It is now Tuesday, and Bill is uneasy as to his position here at St. Jerome's. The Hardwickes are on his mind. Bill's thoughts are now: "What can Bud do to him? What harm can he do to the parish family?" These questions were playing on his mind almost constantly. Bill finally decided not to let Bud bother him to distraction.

At breakfast, Father Joe seemed to be in a very chipper mood. He said, "Bill, remember, Tuesday mornings and Friday mornings are time off for you. I would expect that you might use the time to meet some of the regular people here in town."

Bill was surprised at Father Joe's reminder, and said, "I am delighted to do so, Father. The two incidents from yesterday have been bothering me, however, I am trying not to dwell on them."

Joe continued, "Let me know how it goes. I will want to see that you fit in well with the regulars."

After breakfast, Bill started walking toward the business district to check out what there was to see. He noticed the Mooney's Ice Cream Parlor on Main Street, and took note that the ice cream cones would be a needed item as soon as the weather warms up. Bill turned north on Main Street in front of Mooneys and continued his walk. On the west side of Main, Bill noticed the City Hall/Police

Department building, and behind that was the Fire Department. He also noticed that there was a small group of teens gathered in front of a party store. There was a familiar face in the group. Here was Bart Hardwicke on the street during regular school hours. The whole scene told Bill that Bart was leading a group class skipping effort. Bill walked up to Bart.

"Well, sir, Mr. Hardwicke," said Bill, "I see that you are in the throes of thinking that you are in charge at the school, and of these others. I would recommend that all of you get yourselves up to St. Jerome's High School post haste."

"Well, Father," said Bart, "I don't see your badge showing that you can talk to me like this. I'll go to class when and if I feel like it. Father you're due for an attitude adjustment. You can't come into a new town and be in charge. My granddad won't allow it. He runs this town, and some day, I'll take over for him."

Father Bill was a bit stunned by this display of Bart's bravado. Bill said, "Bart, you must have learned at one point or another, that you should have respect for Christ's priesthood. It is my thought that you should be going to class as scheduled, and to get your work done. I will review your records when I next visit the school."

Father Bill turned away from Bart, and continued his walk north on Main Street. At Elm Street, he paused for a moment to look back toward the party store. He saw that Bart was talking on his cell phone. At any rate, he turned and began walking east on Elm Street. In the middle of the block, there was the huge yellow house with the rounded gables. Bill's impression was that this house could be macabre enough to be the home of a TV monster, or a weird family. Bill suddenly stopped his pace when he noticed the name on the mailbox in front of the ugly house. The name was "Madame Blimpneflah". Bill thought: "So, this is where she lives."

Suddenly, the door swung open, and a chunky woman of about 5 foot 2 inches in height appeared. She had the figure of a bowling pin. She also sported overly dyed black hair which glistened in the sunlight. Madame wore wire rimmed glasses, and a yellow dress that nearly matched her house in color, and torn hose completed the ensemble. She looked straight at Bill while he was sizing up her mailbox. Then, without warning, she went right out to the sidewalk.

Madame said, "Well, of all the nerve for you to be looking at my mailbox. This is private property here. I warned you on the phone not to try to minister here. And, just minutes ago, you were working on Bart Hardwicke just up the street."

Father Bill began, "Madame, I told you that I would minister where ever and when ever I found a need for it. Bart is skipping school, and those of us in charge of St. Jerome's students are responsible for the student's welfare. Namely, they are responsible that the students are in school and that they are kept safe during school hours. If they are not in school they are also responsible to determine if they are ill, or if they are skipping school to the point of record, then they are responsible to take the student and his or her parents into a local court on a truancy charge. Therefore, I am correct in my place to tell him and his buddies to get up to the school right away."

"Hurrumpfh," said Madame, "Bud will no doubt be in touch with you, padre. You can't be serious about what appears to be your personal mission here in Antrim Junction."

Bill replied, "On the contrary, Madame, I am completely serious. I am young and I have the energy to pursue God's children, even you."

Madame's temper was beginning to boil, and she yelled, "Get away, holy Joe, stay away, don't run that holy stuff on me!!"

Madame turned abruptly to walk back to her house and said, quite loudly, "Good day to you, sir!"

Bill resumed his walk sporting a sort of a grin. The grin related to Madame's being quite a challenge to Bill. He noted that she was sort of polite, after all, she called him sir.

Father Bill continued to walk east on Elm Street from his encounter with Madame and her temper. Bill looked up and saw a man standing on the sidewalk, dressed in a black suit, and wearing what appeared to be a chauffeur's cap, complete with the covert looking sunglasses.

The man spoke to Bill, "Father Bill, Mr. Hardwicke would like a word with you."

Bill grimaced, and said, "I would be happy to talk to him."

The chauffeur then directed Bill to a black limo that was parked just up ahead. Bill surmised that this was the same limo that had passed the scene of his first encounter with Vickie. Bill was asked to get into the limo with Bud Hardwicke. Upon entering the car, he was thinking that this car could be a prop in a clandestine movie. He noticed that Mr. Hardwicke was an old man of about 70+ years with graying reddish hair. His face was replete with numerous freckles. He was dressed in 50's style duds with wide lapels.

Bud began, "Well, Father Bill, we meet at last. You have cut quite a wide path here since your arrival. You have crossed paths with a lot of important people in just the few days that you have been here."

Bill replied, "Yes, sir. I am a young and energetic priest who wants to exercise a vocation."

Bud then said, "I understand that, however, this town is my town, mine, and I have put many years into molding it to my liking, and to make it produce much money in the process. I can't have you messing with my set-up. That includes you messing with Bart."

"Bart," Bill began again, "Is skipping school at this very moment, and under the laws of the State of Michigan, we who are in charge of students are responsible for their being in school. Repeated truancies can result in his being taken to a juvenile detention center for up to two months at a time. In this state, the parents and the schools are equally responsible to see that the students are in school."

Bud grimaced, and said, "Father, you will have to overlook that sort of thing with Bart. He will go to school if he feels like it, and he has my support for that."

Bill spoke again, "Well, Mr. Hardwicke, I am an officer of the court when it comes to truancy and I cannot ignore my responsibilities. Bart will have to be in school today, or a report goes in. I will be checking at the attendance office this afternoon. Bart's posture of seeming to run the school has to end as well."

Bud was starting to get plenty steamed at Father Bill, as he felt that Bill is not recognizing his proprietary position in Antrim Junction.

Bud began again, "I am warning you, now, Father, don't rock the boat. you WILL be sorry! Good day to you, sir!"

*Bud and Bart Hardwicke*

## Chapter 10

# "Skirt Boy"

Ian was feeling that things were, at last, settling down. Bart had not hassled him for three days. It is now Friday, a very special day at school, as the students were to address their ethnicity. For Ian, this meant a chance to wear his kilt to school. Such an event was common in Scotland, but here in Antrim Junction there are many different people of separate ethnic backgrounds. It is not an everyday event, but it is twice monthly.

The MacGregor tartan was beautiful, mostly a bright red with criss-crossing black lines forming a lattice pattern with single white lines making larger boxes within the square lattice. Ian always loved this part of his heritage. His kilts meant a lot to him. To his father and brother, the kilts and tartans were way down on their priority lists. Ian's grandfather loved his heritage and Ian deeply respected this. Ian thought: "Grandfather would be proud to see that I can wear this kilt to school in the US."

When Ian got to school he was pleased to see a lot of students dressed in their traditional costumes. One Greek lad was wearing a fustanella, which is a Greek kilt, and there were some German, French, and Spanish costumes to be seen. Ian was pleasantly surprised to see a large number of fellows wearing their kilts in school today.

Ian started to head to his first class, and quite suddenly, his arm was grabbed from the side by someone. Ian looked about to find the source of this interference, finding that, of course, it was Bart.

Bart said, "Well, skirt boy, how are you today?"

Ian was surprised at the snide tone in Bart's voice, and said, "I am just fine, if you don't mind."

Ian yanked his arm away from Bart.

Ian said, "If you please, this is my normal attire for events that are important. I intend to indulge in my heritage where ever I am living."

Bart began again, "Well, Mr. MacGregor, you didn't consult with me for permission to dress like this. Have you already forgotten who runs this school?"

Ian's bravado was beginning to swell, and he said, "For your information, Bart, you do not run all of us, and you can lay off me from now on. I don't come to school here to have my days riddled by your gutless efforts."

Bart was getting steamed that Ian was not cowering to him. He was used to the other kids cowering and submitting to his will, even if it meant that they would be punished for it later.

Bart said, "You haven't heard the last of this, skirt boy, now scram!"

Ian was determined to get in the last word, and said, "Bart, it is you that hasn't heard the last of this!"

Ian stormed off to his first hour class.

Bart didn't understand how he was feeling at this moment. Ian seemed to hold his own with him. He thought: "Was it a victory?" Bart's concentration was broken when he saw Father Bill coming toward him.

Bart said, "Well, Father, how do you like my granddad? I understand that you met him the other day."

Father Bill replied to Bart, "Mr. Hardwicke, it seems that your granddad thinks that he runs this town and its people. I hope that he's getting the message that his vision of his domain is beginning to dissolve. We will vigorously oppose any of his further doings, evil in Antrim Junction must end."

Bart felt himself kind of tripping over his own words as he spoke, "Father, Grandpa Bud will run over you and your friends like a power roller, no survivors. He doesn't like to lose and he will muster every means possible to choke off your efforts. He will also put an end to St. Jerome's if needed."

Bill bristled up at the suggestion and said, "No way, Jose. ~~Change to read~~. The Christ, himself, has placed the two of us priests here and he has given us friends to assist us in the mission. The evil that Bud Hardwicke promulgates here has to stop so the people who live here and built this town can have peace. Now, Bart, off to class with you, I will be reviewing your attendance records this afternoon, with the intention of seeing if there are enough unexcused absences to have you petitioned into court for a truancy hearing. This would involve your parent or guardian, even if that guardian is Bud Hardwicke himself."

"Yes, sir." Bart said, as he walked away from Father Bill. "I'll go to class, but I won't like it."

As Bart departed, Father Bill said to him, "Remember, Bart, my effort here is to bring some peace and quiet to Antrim Junction. This place is quite beautiful, and with peace here, it could be heaven-like."

The morning seemed to go quite well for Ian. The students were enjoying living their heritage. Ian talked with several of the kilted lads, who likewise were happy with the event. Ian felt that their feelings were much like his, and he was glad to feel as good about his heritage as they were. It was nearly noon now, and it was time to go to lunch. It was time to partake of a new gourmet adventure. The school lunches were not what grandma would have cooked up for them.

At the door of the lunchroom, a voice was heard from behind Ian. It was Bart. He said, "Listen here, skirt boy, I have decided that it will cost you a dollar a day to wear that skirt to school each and every time that you do. I run this school, and you can pay the cashier." Bart held out his hand for the payment.

Ian bristled up at the mere suggestion of paying Bart for anything. Ian said, "Bart, you can shove it! I will never pay you for anything in my life. None of your authority, which is assumed, is recognized by me. You can just stay away from me! And Bart, I will wear this kilt anytime I want."

Bart was temporarily stunned. He followed Ian into the lunchroom, now crowded with over three hundred students on their noon break. Ian looked about and noticed that Bart had had second thoughts about pressing him for payment. Many of the other students paused to see if Bart would be so dumb as to start something with Ian during lunch.

Bart, realizing that he needed to back off of Ian, stormed out of the lunchroom and ran right into Father Bill.

Father Bill spoke to Bart, "Bart, I am reviewing your attendance records this afternoon, and I will have some news for you sometime tomorrow. We are conducting a fine tooth exam of them. If there are any anomalies there, we will find them. If we take you to court, it will not be with Judge Stewart hearing the case. It will be sent to the Family Court at the county seat."

Bart exhaled with a sound of disgust for Father Bill. Bart felt that Father Bill was hammering him about researching his records, after all he said this same stuff this morning.

Bart said, "Father, what do you want? You can't hurt me. I am still in charge here. You, Father, are dismissed."

Bill was soundly upset at being dismissed by a kid, and said, "Respect, Bart, respect. You have to learn to respect one's elders, and, of course, priests. It is time to quit bullying the younger lads here. They have the right to attend school in peace. They do not need your uppity treatment. Now, YOU, are dismissed, get to class now!"

Bart turned and left. As Bart walked to his first afternoon class, he passed by Ian in the hallway without the slightest blurb or insult. Ian noticed him but did not go near him. He was puzzled as to why Bart did not take the time to rough him up as usual.

# Chapter 11

## "Ian Meets Bud"

After school was over, Ian was walking back home when a rush of sound was approaching him from behind. Ian turned to see a car coming toward him, kind of fast for this little street. At the wheel was Bart Hardwicke. It seemed as though Bart was trying to scare him with a near miss encounter with his car. Ian got into the clear to watch Bart and his buddies spin past him. They were enjoying themselves immensely as the dutiful lackeys attached to Bart.

Ian's mind was asking: "Is he tying to hurt me? What does he want from me? Why does Bart keep pushing on me, others wore kilts to school today?"

Home was just ahead, and Ian was glad to be there. It is Friday, the weekend is here, and he would not have to run into Bart until Monday.

Just as Ian sat down in the kitchen, he heard his father coming in. Andrew looked tired and in need of a break. He was glad to see his son. He said, "Ian, it's good to see that you have gotten home safely. I saw a car driving up the lane and coming dangerously close to you as you were walking home. I did not like the looks of it."

Ian had been wanting to tell his father about what had been going on at school. Ian spoke, "Father, the driver was Bart Hardwicke.

He's the chap who hassles me almost every day at school. We almost came to fists today when he called me 'skirt boy'. We were supposed to dress according to our heritage today, which I did. Grandfather would have been proud to see the MacGregor kilt going to school in the US this morning. His intense loyalty to his heritage can be seen in me, I hope. There were lots of other guys wearing kilts at school today. I've learned that there's a large Scottish population here in Antrim Junction. So I feel even better about being here."

Andrew quizzed his son, "Is this guy a bully?"

Ian answered his father's question, "Yes, sort of, father, he's the grandson of Bud Hardwicke, who is the self appointed chief of crime here in our town. Bud runs the numbers racket. His employees are those little fellows you see on the street corners carrying well used paper bags. In those bags are the number bet slips and the bet monies. Those guys are waiting for the bookies to pick up the numbers and the money. This is usually in the form of Bud's chauffeur. In his role as kingpin, Bud's influences have rubbed off on Bart, his grandson, and as a result Bart thinks that he runs the students at St. Jerome's High School. I have been at odds with him since day one."

Andrew was clearly distressed upon hearing about Ian's daily hassles. Andrew said, "Ian, what can be done about it? Can't the principal of the school control this guy?"

Ian replied, "Father, Mr. Kelley is a puppet of Bud's. The other day, Father Bill sent the both of us to the office for discipline, and I was the only one who got grilled by him. Bart was let off for the incident. The Hardwickes have a stranglehold on this town. The only people they don't regularly mess with are the two priests. As you may have heard, Father Joe Williams has been kept suppressed by the Hardwickes for many years, keeping him, for the most part, a captive in his own house. He is rarely seen outside in town apart from the church property."

Andrew began again, "Ian, I think that Father Bill may be your best ally in your quest to stifle Bart. If I see Bill, I will suggest that the two of you get together for a chat. I really want this new job and home to work out for us. I feel that the Hardwickes need some form of attitude adjustments."

Ian was reluctant to change his clothes. He loves his kilts. He did give in and changed to blue jeans, tee shirt, sneakers, and he put on a light jacket, and set off for a walk downtown.

He was almost to the center of the business district when he noticed that Bart's car was approaching.

"Skirt boy!" yelled Bart.

Ian did not give into indulging in Bart's escapade. He continued on his walk. Up ahead, he saw that the numbers courier was exchanging the paper bags with the driver of the black limo. Ian was thinking: "Why would the chauffeur be so open about the number exchange? It seems that everyone in town knows the chauffeur and to whom he is attached."

As Ian paused to watch the exchange, he was wondering: "Is there some way to interfere with the numbers and the bet slips and the exchange thereof?"

Ian was aware of the fact that Bud uses the numbers drawn by the Michigan State Lottery. Albert Leslie had advised Ian of much about this sort of thing. Bud gets a lot of business with these numbers because he pays prizes that are $100 more than what the State pays for a winning 4 digit number played straight.

Ian also noticed that Bart's car was parked in front of Mooney's Ice Cream Parlor. After Bart got out of his car, he was looking around to see if any of his lackeys were nearby. After he had collected an array of his chums, Bart was, once again, the center of attraction with them.

Bart was crowing to them, "Did you see skirt boy at school today? Oops, he's right over there, be careful about what you say, he might beat you up."

Ian sensed that he was being belittled by the crowd of boys up ahead. He didn't seem to care. He pushed ahead to go to Mooney's where he purchased a single dip regular cone of French Vanilla. He sat down to enjoy his treat and then noticed that Bart was coming into the store. Bart looked around and spotted where Ian was sitting.

Bart came over, and said, "Ian, I feel that you are not afraid of me or the guys. It seems that you, being new to Antrim Junction don't realize that there are lots of things that go on here that you have to ignore. You have to let things be as they are."

Ian was miffed at this intrusion, and said, "Bart, you are under the mistaken notion that you run the school and the students. Mark my words, it isn't going to last long."

Bart reacted smugly, and said, "You're a pretty big talker for a little guy. Talk is cheap, and do is where it is. Ian, you can get hurt here if you do not snap into line. Granddad will bring you into line. Believe me, you don't want that. Granddad wants things his way, and so do I. I'm following in his footsteps, and I WILL be great."

Ian was not amused, and said, "Bart, it's true that I'm new here. I came here from Scotland and I was uprooted from by beloved fatherland, and with three days notice I was made to come to America. I had to leave many of my things behind. I had to leave my best friend in all the world. I have been mourning about the loss of my homeland for sometime now. Your picking about the kilt was a bit too much. There were many other guys wearing their kilts at school today as well. I have decided to wear it at other times as well. Further, I will not pay you for the privilege of wearing it to school. You must also know that I have been investigating the vices that your Grandpa Bud operates here and I am seeking a way to end them."

Bart was sensing that this conversation with Ian was not going to be productive in a way that he felt was needed.

Bart said, "Ian, I will always be here, and I will always be scouting for granddad, and with the help of Madame, we will keep things going. Madame, as you know, watches over things and coordinates Bud's efforts. Ian you cannot stop the machine, so don't try."

Ian finished up his treat, and said, "Bart, I will make every effort to bring it about just as you will make every effort to stop me. See you around, non skirt boy."

Ian stood up and turned abruptly, and left the Ice Cream Store.

Bart just sat there, amazed once again about Ian's bravado. His thoughts: "Ian is strong, can I prevail? Can we prevail?"

Ian resumed his walk which was ultimately planned to get him back home. Turning east on Elm street, Ian remembered that Madame's house was up ahead. There it was, the huge yellow house with the strange roof. Ian had decided to walk by without pausing. Up ahead, in the middle of the sidewalk was Bud's chauffeur. Ian's pace slowed, but he remained in motion. As Ian was approaching the chauffeur, he felt that something was up with this new situation.

The chauffeur spoke to him, "Sir, Mr. MacGregor, Mr. Hardwicke requires meeting you. He is waiting here in his limo, just up ahead, sir."

Against his better judgment, Ian decided to see Bud. It might as well be now rather than later. Inside the car, Ian saw an old man, who, at one time had red hair, now graying rather profusely. He seemed to, in Ian's estimation, to be a crusty old curmudgeon not wanting to slow down in his elder years.

Bud began, "I am Bud Hardwicke, Mr. MacGregor, I am pleased to meet you at last."

Bud extended his handshake toward Ian. Ian returned the kind gesture and shook Bud's hand.

Bud said, "Mr. MacGregor, I feel that you need to know who I am, and what it is that I stand for here in Antrim Junction. I am an old man now. I have longed for retirement, and I won't have that luxury in the foreseeable future. I run this town. Quite successfully, I might add. Things happen here because I make them happen. If I don't want a certain event, it won't come to pass. You may have gathered that something was different here from your very first moments in town when you met Vickie. She screens out the people who are coming to live here. I knew about you within minutes of your family's arrival at Montrose University. We are pleased to have your father here taking care of our campus grounds and its buildings. It looks great."

Bud continued, "Ian, you must understand that you cannot cause a disruption of things that make Antrim Junction a success for me. You have probably been advised that I run the numbers racket here, and prostitution, and a drug ring. The numbers that I run is a departure from the Michigan State Lottery. They pick the numbers, I pay bigger prizes, and I make the money. As to prostitution, I have only one girl left, and she is getting old, and she has only a few clientele left; her customers are dying off. No drugs left either, as many drugs can be had at chain stores for $4. I make virtually all of my money on the numbers, and I also own several businesses in the downtown area."

"Bart has said to me that you have the intention of trying to stop the numbers here in town. You can not do this, as I will prevail, and I am stronger than you, and I have an elaborate early warning system in place. This is anchored by Madame. She has ten telephone lines in her house to facilitate this effort. I have interference from Henry Horton who owns the phone company. He knows that Madame makes most of the phone calls locally, tying up the lines and keeping others from even getting a dial tone. At present, he is the only one putting up a front against me, that is, until you came here. Of course, there is the new curate at St. Jerome's, he could be a problem."

Ian was surprised that Bud Hardwicke was being so frank with him. Ian said, "Mr. Hardwicke, it's only natural for us to oppose those forces that are evil. The constant betting on numbers with you can only lead to habitual gambling, and I suspect that you indulge persons in betting on other things apart from the numbers."

"Mr. Hardwicke, Father Bill is a wonderful new addition to St. Jerome's staff, and I will be with him as he begins efforts to put an end to the numbers operation. I came here from Scotland just weeks ago, and I have never experienced persons trying to run our lives like we have here. Bart has tried to charge me a dollar a day for the privilege of wearing my kilt to school, and we almost came to fists over that. It is for now, tempered. I loved my fatherland from which I was forcibly removed to come here. I was delighted, just today, to find out that there are many Scots living here, as there were lots of kilts being worn at school today. This makes it a lot easier to be here. My father was fed up with poverty at home, and along with the repeated labor strife in the mines and on the railroads, he decided to bring us here when the chance to become the caretaker at the college was had. Well, Mr. Hardwicke, that is where

I am coming from, and I will help in every way to put an end to the numbers."

Bud was somewhat stunned at Ian's forthrightness on the numbers issue, and said, "Ian, I respect your honesty with me. I understand how you feel. Mark my words, I will resist your efforts, even if it means that some people will get hurt. These people that are betting numbers habitually, are grown adults, and they know what they are doing. It is their business that they bet and not yours. Bart will keep me informed as to what you're doing."

Ian got up to leave the limo, "Good day to you, Mr. Hardwick, I must be getting home."

Bud replied, "Thank you for your time, Ian."

The chauffeur closed the limo door after Ian got out, and then the two of them drove away.

# Chapter 12
## *"Some Nagging"*

Ian was puzzled by the fact that Bud Hardwicke thought that he had to take the time to talk to him personally. Bud was pushy, not as Bart, but polite. Bud seemed to respect Ian's position on the issues at hand.

Ian was about to resume his walk toward the caretaker's house, when he heard a commotion behind him. Turning about, he saw Madame Blimpneflah and Father Bill in the midst of a substantial go around near Madame's mailbox.

Madame was steamed up, and said, "Listen here, holy Joe, you keep your stinking nose out of our business. It will serve to keep you healthy. We will go after you the first time that you attempt to interfere.Padre, you need to stay out of sight and you need to keep a low profile, just like Father Joe does."

Father Bill was quite peeved, and said, "Madame, I fail to see where you fit into this picture, however, I will find out, and maybe when your part is exposed, it may just turn out that it wasn't so cool after all. You can't help but be visible, you have a gaudy yellow, sticks out type house, a big mailbox, and a big mouth."

Father Bill couldn't believe that he had just heard himself say this stuff to Madame. Bill continued, "Madame, all of you involved numbers gurus seem to be joined at the hips, that includes you, Vickie, Bud Hardwicke, Bart Hardwicke, Judge Stewart, the chauffeur, and on and on."

Madame was determined to have the last word with Father Bill, and said, "Hit the road, padre, we will deal with you very soon, and we'll adjust your point of view."

At that, Madame turned abruptly and returned to her house.

Ian approached the site of the exchange with a smirk showing on his face. Ian said, "Father, I saw the whole event with Madame, and I want you to know that I have just had a meeting with Bud Hardwicke. Mr. Bud informed me, in no uncertain terms, that neither you nor I will be able to put a stop to the numbers and all the betting. Bud is betting on all sorts of things, sporting events included, with whom, he feels are his seasoned suckers, confirmed losers. Some of these people are being kept in poverty by the Hardwickes, as I see it. The Hardwickes are extracting their very life blood for the betting. Father, my dad suggested that you and I might be allies in an effort to bring about an end to this betting sickness here in Antrim Junction."

Father Bill was delighted to hear Ian say this. He said, "Ian, tomorrow morning would be a good time for us to get together. How about up at your house at 10AM?"

Ian was now sporting a wide grin, and said, "Yes, Father, I think that would work, and my dad might be able to offer some suggestions. He is a veteran of endurance when it comes to living through strikes and labor strife in Scotland."

"Incidentally, Father, you are a Scot, aren't you?" inquired Ian.

Father Bill was showing a small grimace, and said, "Ian, I do not indulge in heritage. I have bad memories in my past. I cannot seem to overcome some of those bad times, and I have suppressed them. My family's men have never shown much, if any, emotion, showed caring, or basic love. When I told them that I wanted to be a priest, they laughed at me, and put me down. It was quite hurtful. Now here in Antrim Junction, I am experiencing an awakening of some of that lack luster kind of love, as the elements try to run the lives of the people here."

Ian was somewhat startled at what Bill had said, and stated, "Father, you can't let that kind of thing drag down your pride in our fatherland. I love Scotland, and its people, and I am very emotional about the loss of it all. I was brought here really against my will, and I have been made to accept it. Here, I found that there are lots of Scots in residence, and I am beginning to feel at home here. The twice a month Friday dress your heritage day is nice, and very helpful for me. Bart tries to charge me a dollar a day to wear my kilt to school. So, Father, as we get to know each other better, I hope that I can help you to actually be who you are, a Scot!"

Father Bill was taken aback, and said, "Ian, thank you for your comments, it means a lot to me. You are probably right in suggesting that my own pride in heritage should be just that, mine. Till tomorrow morning, Ian, thanks."

# Chapter 13

## *"The First Plans"*

Early Saturday morning, Madame's phone rang. A call was coming in on line nine. Madame, at once, knew who was calling. Of course, it was Henry Horton.

Madame answered the phone, and said, "Hello."

The caller said, "Good morning to you Madame, Henry Horton here. I just wanted to remind you that maybe, in your kindness, you could cut back on your calls this weekend. Maybe it would benefit other phone customers who could possibly get a dial tone for once."

Madame had not had breakfast yet. Being a bit edgy, she replied, "Horton, you jerk, I will make as many calls as I want. I pay for each and every one of them, should it matter to you? Further, I am paying for ten lines each month, as well as for all of those ancillary charges that you phone types proffer."

Henry continued, "Madame, there is no need to get hostile. We are all residents of a small town and we all share in the limited capabilities of a small town phone company. I am just trying to help all of us to be able to make our calls. Have a nice weekend, Madame, good bye."

Madame now felt that she needed her first morning coffee, and she set about to brew it up to her special liking. After a few sips of the unique concoction, she clicked on the hot line, line ten to be exact, to call Bud Hardwicke. She could hear the phone ringing and, as always, she was able to count the five rings before Bud would answer.

Madame said, "Good morning, Bud, Madame Here."

Bud Hardwicke was surprised that he was receiving the hot line call this early in the day. Bud said, "What is so urgent that you would bother to call this early?"

Madame was a bit startled at Bud's retort, she said, "Yesterday, Friday, I had two go arounds with the new people in town. First with the lad, Ian, and secondly with Father Bill. I must admit that the two of them enraged me, and I shot off my mouth to them!"

Bud was sporting a smile unseen by Madame, and he said, "Madame, I trust that you will keep your cool until such time that they make their first move. I have spoken to each of them privately. I have informed them of their place here, and that we will not tolerate interference. I think that I at least have the attention of Ian, although that could change if the two of them get together. I understand that there have been at least two instances of exchange between the two of them at school and one at the church."

Madame added, "That may well be the case, but I can not trust either of them. The padre yelled at me that I have a big mouth. That was just the first level of insults coming from a Scot. These Scots, as you know, are genetically bullheaded, stubborn, and come equipped with acid tongues. Their comments are often barbed, designed to irritate."

Bud was amused at Madame's reactions, and said, "My dear Madame, you need to calm down, and have less coffee this early in the morning, or is it Irish coffee already today?"

Madame grimaced, but she managed to be polite, and said, "Bud, I will watch them closely, and I will keep you informed. If alerted by Bart, I will coordinate with you immediately."

"Good day to you, Madame," Bud said as he hung up.

Over at the caretaker's house, one could see that Father Bill was approaching in a leisurely stroll to have his meeting with the MacGregors. Bill was noticing that spring is, indeed, here. The numbers of birds is visibly on the increase. Songbirds were singing a happy spring song. God's world seemed to be quite beautiful today, as Bill, for once, took the time to notice all the things that the Creator has made right here in front of him. Bill looked at his watch, it was now 9:50AM, and looking up, he was nearing the MacGregor's residence, the caretaker's house.

In a few minutes, Bill could see Ian coming toward him. Bill said, "Good morning, Ian, what a beautiful day."

Ian was glad to see Bill walking up, and he observed that Father Bill was dressed as a civilian. Without the priestly uniform, Bill looked just like any other guy on the street.

Ian said, "Hi, Father, welcome, come on in."

The two of them entered the house and went directly to the kitchen. It is in the kitchen, around the dinner table, that most Scots do their family talking.

Ian said, "Sit down Father, and make yourself at home, please feel like it is also your home."

Bill began, "Thanks, I already sense an infusion of heritage coming my way. It's OK. My feeling is that we have to stop Bud Hardwicke in his tracks. This will be a first step in bringing peace and calm to Antrim Junction. I wouldn't have believed it if told to me at the outset that I would dive into this town with such gusto, and with such a desire to make things better here."

Father Bill began again, "Ian, let's, as Bishop Sullivan once said to me, "Let's cut through the crap and get down to the meat of the subject." By that, I mean that I want you to call me Bill in the informal setting like we have here. It is important so that we can experience the family feeling that you so desperately want."

Ian smiled, and said, "Thanks, Bill, I hope that our efforts will get us somewhere toward our peaceful goal. At my level, it is Bart who is the raspberry seed under a denture. At your level, the enemy is Bud and Madame. Just how to cope with this is unknown."

Just then, Andrew entered the kitchen, and said, "Good morning, Father Bill, I am delighted that you have come to our home. Welcome."

Bill rose to shake Andrew's hand. Andrew was pleased that Bill was so polite. Andrew indicated that all of them should sit down.

Bill began, "Andrew, Ian and I have been discussing the problem that we all share in Antrim Junction, namely the rampant betting on illegal numbers. We have just began to explore the possibilities of interfering with Bud's main project."

Ian felt the need to interject here, and he said, "Yesterday, I met Bud Hardwicke and talked with him in the back of his limo. This took place on Elm Street, just east of Madame's house. It seems, according to Bud himself, that the numbers racket is the main item in his repertoire, as he said that he has only one prostitute, and she is getting old and her customers are dying off. Walmart is selling some drugs for $4, an event that put him out of the drug business. I think that he owns a few businesses down town that are legit. Stopping the numbers racket won't put him into the poorhouse. He would just have to earn his money honestly."

Bill said, "Thanks, Ian, that is much more info than I was able to get out of him. You are also right on the key point that I represent much more of a threat to his efforts than you do. He did not, however, think that the two of us would ever be allied against him."

Andrew added, "Listen guys, in order to get law enforcement involved here, we would have to go to the outside for assistance. The local police department is under the control of Bud Hardwicke, namely in the form of Chief Dudley Hardwicke. Dudley is Bud's brother. This means, here in Michigan, that we must involve the State Police. You will have to go down to Kalkaska to get their assistance. You will probably have to meet with the post commander to make some sort of a plan with him. They can back you up so that no one gets hurt."

Bill smiled and said, "Andrew, I completely agree, but first, I think that we need to siphon off some of the money locally by some means of fund raising. Some of the priests that I know have already conducted a parish raffle with a cash prize. This may be the way to go. If we score with the people using a raffle resulting in Bud's take that week being reduced, it may make a point to him. We have to crawl before we can run."

"An excellent idea," said Andrew, "If we can promote the raffle with say, a $500 cash prize, some of the bettors may just turn their attention to this for just one week. It has some very good possibilities. A few second prizes would also be needed."

Bill was ready with a reply, "Yes, yes, maybe a couple of $100 gift certificates to the local department store. Maybe a trial membership at a gym. There are lots of things that we can do. I feel that we need to start slowly so that Bud will notice but not be alarmed."

Ian was getting excited about the idea of sticking it to Bud, but mostly to Bart. Ian said, "Let's do it. This will be fun. Bill, what can he do to us in retaliation?"

Bill was also prepared with a negative note, and said, "Ian, I once heard it noted that there was a test for this. It consisted of two questions. First, can this guy put me on the night shift? And, secondly, can this guy cut my work hours? If the answers were no to both, then full speed ahead. Ian, I doubt if the Hardwickes are brazen enough to commit physical injury to any of us. After all, there are many more of us than there are of them. The answer to both questions is no, so off we go."

Ian was a bit relieved, and said, "Father, what do you think?"

Andrew was pleased that he was included, and he said, "Ian, it is necessary that the illegal numbers be squashed. Some of the people that I have met here in town are always broke because of their betting on the numbers with Bud. Bud will also bet on almost anything, always seeming to win."

Ian smiled, and said, "Father, it is so cool that we can go ahead with this, and maybe the peaceful town that we want is just outside of our window. If we can help bring it about, it will feel just as good as being in Scotland."

Andrew was feeling a gush of pride in his youngest son, and said, "Ian, your granddad would have burst through his buttons seeing you in this effort. MacGregors and MacKenzies together in a common effort. Who would have thought that would be possible here in the US? The US has to begin to be our home, and why not start now?"

The three of them visited with much small talk until Father Bill discovered that he should return to the church for the vigil Mass preparations.

# Chapter 14

## "The Raffle Begins"

After Mass on Saturday, which was a vigil Mass for the next day, being Sunday, Ian was not in a hurry to leave the church. He found himself talking to some of the local folks on the veranda.

The chatter was all about the upcoming parish raffle which was announced by Father Bill after Mass. It seems that the tickets would sell for $1 each with a maximum of ten tickets per person. The 1st prize was $500 in cash, the 2nd prize was a $100 gift certificate for grocery shopping at the local IGA store, south of the City Limits. the 3rd prize was a certificate for 10 tickets in the next parish raffle at St. Jerome's.

Father Bill was right, Ian thought, as the interest in the raffle had been keen. After all, the profit from the raffle would go to support summer sports for the kids from the parish grade school.

Father Bill was all smiles as he walked among his people gathered outside. He was obviously pleased at what he saw. In most big city parishes, the people scrammed right after the Mass ended. Not here, as it seems that the parish family feeling is beginning to happen.

After the crowd began to thin out, Ian and Father Bill walked toward each other. Bill said, "Ian, what did I tell you? This has made a significant impression on the folks here. It is a first assault on Bud's master plan. Some of these people will turn to the raffle as a replacement for the numbers, even though it is for just one week. It will show Bud that there is something that can be done."

Ian grinned, and said, "Bill you can be sure that I will hear from Bart soon. He will be beside himself thinking that his future inheritance of Bud's businesses will be in jeopardy."

Bill wanted to remind Ian to be cautious, and said, "Ian, remember that we have to crawl before we can run, and taking it easy is the byword. Do not lean into punches. You are known to be against the illegal numbers, and you can rely on the fact that you will be watched by the dynamic three, Madame, Vickie, and Bart. Bud will know what each of us is doing most of the time."

"Madame, as you know, steers the effort, and with Bart watching out constantly, and Vickie running interference, it will be difficult to get anything past them."

Ian, for a moment, was needing to cope with the vastness of the crime machine that they were starting to go up against. Ian said, "Bill, just how big is their crime machine?"

Bill replied, "Well, the police Chief is none other than Dudley Hardwicke, who, just by his name, you can tell is attached to Bud, Bud's brother. Judge Stewart is in the puppet category as his chair spins around whenever Bud coughs. The mayor is Richard Leslie, a small man who goes about town proving to all that he has no clue as to what is going on in town."

Ian was showing some surprise, he said, "Bill, during one of my first walks about town, I met Albert Leslie, who was polishing a stop sign on Elm Street at the Service Drive. He took it upon himself to brief me about all of these guys. Some of what you just said confirms what Albert has told me."

Bill replied, "Ian, I believe that what I have outlined here is just the tip of the iceberg. There must be much more to it. Keep in mind, they won't show all unless tricked into it. Let's let it ride, as a player of roulette might say, and see what flushes out."

Ian smiled, "OK, Bill, it'll be interesting. I'm sure that Bart will speak to me at school early on Monday. I have been playing with his mind, in the sense that he might want to be able to do something for his future if the numbers racket doesn't come his way. He is concerned, but thinking."

Bill smiled, "Good move, Ian, if it messes with his limited thought processes, then it may serve as a lever with him. Any good strategist will tell you, dividing to conquer is a viable approach."

Ian grinned, and said, "Bill, I'm not afraid of Bart. He has a sharp bite sometimes, but he seems to be a bit of a donkey at other times. I can handle him. He even admitted to me that he senses that I will not back down from him and that no one has ever stood up to him before. Incidentally, Father, do you have a kilt here?"

Father Bill grimaced, and said, "Next question."

Ian sensed a soft spot with Father Bill, "Come on, Bill, a good Scot has a kilt handy. Bill it IS your heritage, you canna undo your heritage. Be proud and stand up for it."

Bill was definitely perturbed at Ian's insistence on the kilt issue, and said, "Ian, I have never felt an urge to address my heritage. My younger years were spent living with a father who never showed emotion, and was, what we called the great stone face. I can't remember ever seeing that MacKenzie plaid as it applied to him. It was not a big deal, ever."

Ian was determined, and said, "Do you have a kilt here?"

Bill finally answered him, saying, "Yes, Ian, I do, I have only worn it once, and it hangs in my closet, unused."

Ian, now smiling, said, "Father William MacKenzie, I will keep working on you. Be proud, be who you are."

Bill was now ready to move on, and said, "OK, Ian, if you say so, it will take some doing for me, but you are very convincing."

The two of them parted with each of them going their separate ways.

# Chapter 15

# *"Kevin Calls"*

Ian spent a peaceful weekend. He was able to take it easy and enjoy the day of rest that Christ gave to all of us. Ian had attended the vigil Mass on Saturday evening along with his father and his brother Eric.

Now it was time to go back to school. He decided to test Bart this morning, so he put on his kilt for the day. The walk to St. Jerome's High School was quite enjoyable. The spring feeling was getting stronger and one could hear the insects and the critters making their happy sounds.

Upon arrival at the school, Ian used the main entrance. He looked about expecting Bart to be at the ready. Bart was not at his station of command, his absence noted. Maybe Bart, his main pest, wouldn't be here today.

Moving up the main hall, Ian could see where Bart was being occupied. He could also see that Father Bill was right in the middle of the action, right in Bart's face.

Father Bill said, "Bart, I have talked to you twice before about respect, and I am telling you one last time that I demand respect for myself and for Father Joe, and all of the elders in your life!"

Bart stammered, and said, "But Father Bill, I simply addressed you as Bill. That can not be considered disrespectful."

Bill replied, "I must insist that unless a priest asks to be addressed by his first name, then you are to address him simply as "Father". There are folks here in town to whom I extend this privilege and you are not one of them."

Bart, grimacing, replied, "OK, Father, just as you say."

Bart turned to his right and noticed that Ian was standing there taking the entire event and placing it into his memory.

Bart said, "Well, if it isn't skirt boy, aren't you cute today?"

Ian was clearly miffed at the insult, and said, "Stuff it Bart. I have already informed you that I will wear my kilt whenever I want to and your permission will not be asked, nor needed. Additionally, you would do well to mind your own business as you might find it necessary some day soon to retreat."

Bart was seeing that Ian was not going to back down. Bart said, "Get to class, Ian. I don't have the time to deal with your problem at this time."

Ian was now being loud, and shouted, "Bart, it is time for YOU to get to class, so clear out!"

Bart was startled that the little fellow, as he felt that Ian was to him, has the bravado to address him in that manner. He was sporting a small smile as he moved toward his first hour class, his attendance at which would be a banner waving event for his teacher.

Father Bill spoke up as he again was between Bart and Ian. Father Bill said, "Ian, please report to the conference room. I will join you there in just a few minutes." Turning to Bart, he said, "Now, off with you."

At the conference room, Father Bill sat down with Ian. Father Bill said, "Ian, I realize that you want to stick it to Bart, but you can't bait him like you did this morning. We will, very soon, have some medicine for him. The license for the parish raffle will be here by mid-week and then we can look to do some hassle of our own. The raffle will be directed at the habitual bettor and it will encourage them to be thrifty by placing a limit on the number of tickets that they can buy."

Ian was glad to hear that Father Bill has been working on the proposed raffle ever since the Saturday meeting at the caretaker's house. Ian said, "Father Bill, I will control myself with Bart, and I will let him get himself into trouble. It will probably be an event in which Bart and his assistants will expose themselves to the State Police."

Father Bill, needing to return to his office, said, "I have to get to work, and so do you. Get on to class and I will talk with you later on."

Ian replied, "Aye, sir, Father."

Ian was in the process of gathering up his things for class when Elise came into the conference room. Elise said, "Ian, you have a phone call. The caller told me that he is calling from Scotland. You can take the call in my office."

Ian was a bit puzzled as he made his way to Elise's office. He sat down as directed, at took the call.

The voice on the phone said, "Ian, is that you? This is Kevin."

Ian was delighted at the call, and said, "Kevin, it's so great to hear your voice. I have missed you so much these last few weeks. I have yet to form any solid friendships here in Antrim Junction, although there is a small gang that will do everything that they can to make life miserable here at St. Jerome's High School. What brings your call to this particular phone?"

Kevin started, "Ian, I have missed you a lot. I have wanted to talk to you so much that your father gave me your home phone number and the number at the school and sent them here by post. I am already home from school and I will be going to bed soon. I knew that the time difference would probably put you at school at this time. so I called you and as luck would have it, you were in the office at the time of the call. The reason that I called is to tell you that I will visit you in May. I have won a plane passage and a week vacation in the US. I will write to you about the specific dates and ask you about how to find you. I am so excited about seeing you."

Ian was sporting an uncontrollable grin, and said, "Kevin, I want you to come here, I can hardly wait!"

The two pals proceeded to exchange addresses that were current and ended their call.

For the rest of the day, Ian was on a natural high as he had heard his best friend's voice, now being about five weeks here in Antrim Junction. The anticipation of Kevin's visit was filling Ian's mind with endless possibilities.

In the lunchroom at the noon break, Ian was expecting another set-to with Bart, but strangely enough, it seemed that Bart was not present. He then set about to get his food and to enjoy his break. He had good things to think about.

Too soon, though, Bart approached his table, and sat down. How amazing. Bart said, "Ian, hello. I've been thinking about you quite a bit in the last 24 hours and I have concluded that you are a different sort of chap. One that won't back down if confronted and one that will stand up to me. I've never seen anyone here at school that would stand up to me. I'm a fellow that is looking to take over granddad's businesses when he retires. I have worked lookout for a long time. As you already know, I report to Madame, who coordinates efforts with my granddad, and together we keep things going here."

Ian was feeling that now is the time to educate Bart. Ian said, "Bart, the things that Bud Hardwicke does are morally wrong, and illegal. You would do better if you would direct your attention elsewhere, and learn a viable vocation. One that will lead to a lifetime of fulfillment."

"Bart, have you ever felt that you could do humanitarian things? Possibly caring for elderly people, helping them to live as normal a life as can be had? Could you feel called to be a teacher, a priest, an engineer, a doctor, a nurse? There are a lot of possibilities."

Bart was suddenly feeling low, hearing Ian speak like this, giving forth a feeling of happiness and faith in the future.

Bart said, "I've never known anyone who felt that they could say these things to me. I've never thought about the future, other than being a successor to my granddad. You're right, I do need to think about things if that doesn't come to pass. I would be up the creek."

Ian was feeling that he was, at last, breaking into Bart's world. Ian said, "Bart, life can be better, even here in Antrim Junction, if we all pull together, and put some effort into it."

Ian added, "I haven't decided on a career to pursue yet, but, I'm taking classes that are basic for a lot of areas. The math, the English, and history. Just getting good grades in these classes is important to me now. And, by the way, Bart, kilts are cool."

# Chapter 16

# "Under The Skin"

Monday had arrived again, and Ian was getting ready to go to school. The uniform of the day was faded blue jeans, black tee shirt, sneakers, and a light jacket. The walk to school was uneventful. Ian noticed that the squirrels were chasing around, up and down the tree trunks in their annual mating ritual. The stock answer that they are just playing is obviously incorrect as this game is going on all over the wooded areas.

Upon arrival at St. Jerome's High School, Ian was glad to see that Bart was not waiting form him. However, the prospect of not seeing him was soon to be dashed. Bart could be seen coming toward the main entrance. Bart saw Ian.

Bart said, "Ian, over here, now!"

Ian was surprised that Bart was shouting orders at him this morning. Ian said, "What's up?"

Bart began a tirade, "Ian, you know just what is up. You know about the church raffle and all that goes with it. This raffle has already caused the numbers to drop off. We can't have this. Granddad is quite upset and I would not be surprised if you see the black limo on the streets today."

Ian was sporting a fine Scottish smirk, and said, "Imagine that,

Bart. What do you think that Bud will want to do about it? It seems that his palm may just be getting sweaty, causing his grip on his regular bettors to slip."

This remark by Ian has caused Bart's face to redden with anger. Bart began again, "Ian, you rile me. I am pointing out that my gut feeling is that you are on a steering committee along with Father Bill. You know full well what is going on here. What does the draining of numbers money have to do with you?"

Ian began again, "Bart, I told you some time ago that the betting on numbers and betting in general is morally wrong. Why? Because it violates the laws of the State of Michigan. The numbers set up here is designed to extract the maximum dollars from the bettors, and thus it contributes to keeping these families in poverty. The whole thing stinks."

Bart was seeing that this line of conversation with Ian was turning back on him. Bart said, "Ian, classes will start in a few minutes, I'll talk to you later."

Ian, with a grin, said, "OK, non skirt boy."

Bart stormed off. He'll probably treat his first hour teacher with the luxury of his presence. Ian watched Bart proceed north along the main hallway and away from him. He was thinking: "This church raffle is already getting to him, yes."

Bart's mood in the early morning helped to make the morning go well for Ian. A couple of tests already taken and yet Ian was feeling quite good about things in general. As he sat down in the lunchroom for his noon break, Father Bill came in and sat down with him.

Ian smiled, and began, "Well, Father, Bart is quite steamed, and he warned me that I shouldn't be surprised to see that black limo on the streets today. I suspect that Bud will be calling on some of his regular bettors trying to drum up some business."

Bill was delighted and said, "Ian, that is good news. I hope it continues to torment Bart, and that he will continue to feel pressure from both Bud and Madame."

Ian felt that is was necessary to tell Father Bill an important tidbit. He said, "Father, Bart did tell me that he feels that I am on the steering committee for this assault on the numbers operation. So, I think that talking during lunch and in the open like this is not a very good idea for a while."

Bill grimaced, and said, "Yes, Ian, you are quite correct. I'll contact you later at your home."

Father Bill got up and left the lunchroom. When he arrived at the rectory, Father Joe was waiting for him in the dining room, where he was eating his lunch. As Bill sat down, the housekeeper brought in his lunch.

Father Joe began, "Father Bill, I received a call from Madame just about an hour ago. She is beside herself with anger, if you can imagine the space she could occupy if she could do that. She screeched into the phone at me regarding the raffle that is underway at the parish. It's upsetting the flow of things in town. I told her that it's too bad, and further, Bill, I was surprised at myself for saying that sort of thing to her."

Father Bill was sporting an immense grin, and said, "Father Joe, I am delighted that such unrest has gotten to her already. It's true that our intention is to siphon off part of the regular numbers money to the parish sports fund. The intention is to distract the habitual bettors from Bud's numbers over to a worthwhile raffle which has a betting limit. Some of the families whose monies are drained away by Bud will have some grocery money this week."

Father Joe was obviously pleased with Bill's efforts.

Joe began to speak, "I'm looking for nothing but good to come from this event. For far too long, Bud has kept a number of families in poverty with this betting. He lets them win once in a while, to keep them hooked, and then he bleeds them unmercifully. I'm also pleased as to how fired up Madame seems to be. She could use some means of expending calories."

Father Bill was pleased at hearing these positive remarks from Father Joe. He said, "Father Joe, it seems that Ian and I are targeted as the steering committee and they are quite correct. Ian suggested at lunch, today, that we should not be seen conversing in the open. So, I plan on calling at the caretaker's house later in the day. Bart also warned Ian that the black limo will be roaming about the town today. As you know, Bud likes to do his own hatchet work from the back seat of his limo."

Father Joe was now smiling and said, "Just be careful Bill. We can't have you getting hurt here. Bishop Sullivan will be calling on us this Saturday and he will celebrate the vigil Mass here. This is not generally known. He wants to surprise the people by being here in person."

Father Bill was taken aback by this news, and said, "He already wants to check up on us? We're just getting started in our effort to give Antrim Junction a new infusion of the living Christ. I hope he sees that positive effects are already bringing smiles to the faces that have been sad for such a long time. I'm in love with this ministry, it is, quite correctly, a challenge just as Bishop Sullivan had predicted."

Father Joe smiled, and said, "Bill, don't let the fact of the Bishop being here change any of your plans in this effort. He feels that a stronger presence of the Bishop is warranted throughout the diocese. He's really a good Bishop, and we are lucky to have such a dedicated prelate."

Father Bill smiled, and said, "Father, I'm pleased to receive him here. He's our shepherd. And, as you say, he is in need of seeing the people who are everyday faithful Catholic Christians."

Father Joe smiled, and said, "Until supper time. I'll see you later, Bill."

Father Joe returned to his work leaving Bill in the dining room to reflect on the events of the day.

# Chapter 17

# "Bud Gets Riled"

After school, Ian was feeling like experiencing spring to a greater degree. After he had put his school equipment in the dining room at home, Ian left for downtown. In the back of his mind was the fact that this good feeling is drawing him in a beeline to Mooney's Ice Cream Parlor, and that, today, the double dip fudge walnut ice cream is definitely in jeopardy.

When Ian got inside the entry of Mooney's he noticed that Bart was sitting across the room from him. Ian purchased his cone and found a place to sit. As he began to attack his treat, Bart came over. Bart said, "Ian, may I join you?"

Ian, with a smile, said, "Yes, please, what's going on Bart?"

Bart was kind of choking on his own words, and said, "After you leave here, Bud will find you for a chat. I just thought that I should alert you. The church raffle has wrenched most things for the Hardwickes. Bud is moving about town talking to his regulars and finding out that the discovery of a limit on betting dollars is helping them out. The regulars, some of whom were betting up to $50 a week are saying that they bought a $10 bet on the raffle, which is 10 tickets, and therefore, they feel that they are done with betting for this week."

Ian took a break from his treat as Bart said, "Ian I can't believe that you were right. I must appear to be stuck in this rut. I must look like a prize dope. I am, for now, having to serve the system. Granddad will be calling on me soon and I'll have to be ready to respond."

Ian was surprised that Bart was being so frank about the situation. He said, "Bart, be careful, don't end up being a patsy for the system. Back away gracefully if you have to."

Bart stood up, and looking about, said, "Ian, thanks for understanding. The black limo just went past the shop. He's heading north on Main Street, See you later."

With that, Bart left Mooney's.

Ian was reflecting upon what had just happened between Bart and himself and smiled. The plan, in just its infancy, was beginning to upset the crime machine in Antrim Junction.

After Ian had finished his treat at Mooney's, he began to walk north on Main Street. This had become his regular walking route. Soon, there would be the right turn onto Elm Street. This would take him past Madame's house. Just as he approached the gaudy yellow house, the door flew open, and the enraged bulk of Madame Blimpneflah burst upon the porch.

Madame yelled, "You there, MacGregor, stop where you are! You must not move another inch until I talk to you."

Ian was now almost frozen in his path, and said, "As you wish Madame."

Ian watched as Madame waddled out to her mailbox site.

Madame said, "MacGregor, you are walking on thin ice. You are helping that holy Joe to bring a church raffle to Antrim Junction. I'm warning you to knock it off. We will not tolerate this interference in our routine here."

Ian was wanting to get moving along, and said, "Well, Madame,

I can not remember when I have had a better time than this little chat of ours. I wish you well and I hope that you will control your blood pressure. Good day, Madame."

Madame turned suddenly, and began to head back to her porch. During this time, she signaled the chauffeur who was waiting on the sidewalk just east of her house.

When Ian neared the chauffeur, he realized that he could not avoid the meeting with Bud Hardwicke. So, upon making eye contact with the chauffeur, he moved toward the limo. The door swung open, and the voice from inside said, "Get in!"

While Ian was getting seated in the limo, he could see that, without a doubt, Bud was bent out of shape.

Ian offered, "Hello, sir."

Bud began, "Ian, I have talked with you before and I felt, at that time, that you would be a problem to the operation of things here in Antrim Junction. There is no need to review with you the facts of the last 48 hours. The regular bettors have dropped back, saying that they are betting on the raffle this week. They are not interested in betting with me, even though I have offered an extra $100 premium on the prizes. That is, as you know a full $200 more than what the State pays."

Ian was feeling a gush of bravado, and he said, "Mr. Hardwicke, you must realize that your crime wave is destined to end. These things cannot live on forever. It is time to let up on your machine. It is time for Antrim Junction to become the peaceful rural college town that it can be. Peace is a gift of the living Christ, and you need to take in some of it for yourself."

Bud's temperament is getting increasingly irate. He said, "I will not allow you or Father Bill to change things here. I will take steps to put an end to your efforts. Vickie will be watching you quite closely and you could even get arrested. Vickie is the senior police officer here. She will not let the slightest thing go by."

Ian was beginning to stir as he was seeing a need to exit this situation. Ian said, "Mr. Hardwicke, do what you must, but evil cannot and will not prevail. We will pluck your bones of money until this is over, and you lose! Good day to you sir."

Ian left the limo at this point, and spoke to Bud's chauffeur, "You are dismissed."

The rest of the way home Ian was sensing that someone or something was behind him. Turning around, he saw that the cop car was pacing his walk. In the car, of course, was the extra rotund Vickie. Vickie was the constable on patrol at this time.

Ian decided to slow his pace so that the cop car would come up directly beside him.

When the cop car was aligned with Ian, he turned to Vickie and said, "Vickie, how nice to see you again. What a lovely day for a walk and to receive verbal assaults from two criminals."

Vickie was not amused, and she said, "Well, MacGregor, I have been advised that you are being disruptive on your way today. Possibly you need to come downtown to be interviewed by our beloved Chief of Police, Dudley Hardwicke."

Ian was clearly riled at Vickie's intrusion into his day, and he said, "Vickie, you can go jump into a lake. Wow, what a scene that would be. I know that you have to have probable cause to detain me. You have not even a glimmer of an idea as to what that would require. Further, I know that in order to arrest me, that you have to witness a felony being committed in your presence. So buzz off, and let me be. I'm on my way home."

Vickie retorted, "Ian, I will be watching you very carefully. Don't step over the line and get noticed."

Ian's bravado was growing, and he said, "Yes, your royal fatness."

Ian turned and resumed his walk home. Ian had just realized now that he had antagonized Vickie, and that he will, indeed, be a target for her.

When Ian arrived home, he went to the kitchen, and there he found his father, and believe it nor not, Eric was home, and there in the kitchen.

Ian said, "Eric, wow, you're here. Maybe I should call the newspaper and give them the scoop."

Eric was not amused, and said, "Ian you are getting a sharp tongue on you. I don't need to hear your kiddie insults in our own house."

Ian began again, "Eric, we've been here in the US for several weeks, and it's about time that you were doing something for yourself. Even Americans look down on lounge lizards, non workers, etcetera. You could get a job. You could volunteer until a new semester starts at the college. You qualify for free tuition at Montrose University. You can get a viable degree here."

Eric began to speak, now louder than before, "Ian, shut up. I will find a job. It's just that I haven't found a job that would suit my training and previous experience."

Ian knew that he had, once again, gotten under Eric's skin with his barbed comments. Ian just sat there grinning at Eric. Ian said, "Eric, there's no market for a professional that sits on one's ass."

"Remarks like that will get yours kicked, Ian," an irate brother blurted, "Get off my case and I will show you that I can be productive."

Ian said in reply, "You don't have to prove yourself to me. But you do need to be a producing member of the population here.

Father will be proud of you if you're busy with some sort of a goal in life."

"Just tone it down, Ian," said Eric, "Things will improve. I'm looking at a job right now at Mooney's."

Ian, smiling, said, "OK, big guy."

Andrew was taking in all of this exchange between his sons in silence. He finally spoke, "The two of you need to calm things down between you. There will be much change of paces here in Antrim Junction very, very soon. It's time that harmony at home was a part of the effort."

Ian then went to his room and began to watch his TV. He was glad that the evening will furnish some relaxation and some time for thought.

# Chapter 18
## "Bishop Sullivan Comes To Town"

Saturday had arrived without any further encounters with either Bud, Madame, Bart, or Vickie. This afternoon, after the vigil Mass, the parishioners of St. Jerome's and their friends will gather in the high school gym for the drawing of the winning raffle tickets.

Bart had informed Ian that there was a dramatic drop in the betting traffic for the week. While Bud's temperament was tentative, it was felt that he would get over it. Ian, however, thought that it would be a good idea to talk to Father Bill before the Mass, possibly in the hour or so.

After two telephone attempts to reach Father Bill, an answer was had on the third try. Ian said, "Father Bill, Ian here, do you suppose that we should talk before you get busy with the vigil Mass preparations?"

Father Bill replied, "Yes, Ian, of course, but where shall we meet?"

Ian was ready, and said, "Bill, let's meet in the picnic grove on the campus. My father and his crew have made it quite nice for the new season's use."

Bill said, "Is 11 O'clock OK?"

Ian replied, "Yes, quite, see you then."

The call ended.

At the picnic grove there was a definite improvement visible. Everything was properly in place. The grills had been repaired and made ready to sacrifice hot dogs.

Bill MacKenzie had a penchant for being on time, and therefore, arrived at the picnic grove precisely at 11AM. Ian was a few minutes behind the padre.

Ian had arrived, saying, "Hi Father, how are you?"

Bill turned, and at the sight of a smiling Ian, he said, "I am peachy fine, and may I say that you are looking dapper today? Are you feeling good?"

Ian was all grins, and said, "Yes, sir, I am well. The tone of things all about town is positive, and I love it."

Bill was happy to see that Ian's demeanor was much improved. Bill said, "Ian, there is a surprise for you and most of the people in the parish today. His eminence, the Most Reverend Joseph Sullivan, Bishop of Evart will celebrate the vigil Mass this evening. Are you surprised?"

Ian was, indeed, surprised, and said, "Why is he coming here today? According to folks that I have talked to, he has never, in their recollection, ever been here at St. Jerome's"

Bill replied, "You are quite right, Ian. The good Bishop will be here to witness the new found happiness that he has heard about. And you are also correct with the inference that it is about time that he made an Episcopal visit to this parish."

Ian began again, "Bill, will he get hassled when he gets into town? You most certainly did, as did my father."

Bill said, "Well, Ian, you know that Vickie is lurking about, especially since your meeting with Bud up on Elm Street earlier this week."

Ian was smiling, and said, "You're right, she's on the lookout for me. I addressed her as her royal fatness when she was pacing my walk back home after I met with Bud Hardwicke. I intentionally slowed my pace so that the cop car would come up directly beside me, so that a face to face confrontation could be had. And after a suitable amount of hassle, she prepared to leave, and then I insulted her."

Bill was amused, and said, "Good job. I was steamed up when she ticketed me on my first day here. A sixty dollar ticket resulted, courtesy of Judge Stewart, who ruled according to Bud's wishes. Judge Stewart left the bench to make a phone call and then came back to announce my fine of $60. After this experience, I have used hindsight to muse about being that brave with her myself back then, but alas, hindsight has twenty-twenty vision."

Ian noticed that it was almost noon, and said, "Father we need to break off here, so that we each can catch our lunch break. I'll go downtown to decoy Vickie if that's possible. You have to prepare for the Bishop's Mass at 5PM. Well, maybe I can divert Vickie's attention long enough for the Bishop to come into town without being noticed."

Bill said, "Good luck on that. I'll see you after Mass."

The meeting ended with each of them going on their own for lunch.

After lunch, at about 2PM, Ian decided that it was time to go downtown and check up on Vickie. While approaching Mooney's, Ian noticed that Bart was his buddies were already in place at the harassment stand. Bart looked reinvigorated and ready to tangle with someone.

It was a small task for Ian to approach Mooney's. He looked straight ahead. Ian said, "Hello, Bart, what's cooking?"

Ian was suddenly personally amused as he realized that he was saying some American lingo to his nemesis.

Bart replied, "We're on watch today. The winner of the St. Jerome's raffle will be drawn after this afternoon's Mass. Granddad is quite bent out of shape over it. He'll probably be at the gym after Mass. The limo has passed by here several times today. You can count on him to know who the winner is, and he or she will get a barrage of temptation to keep on betting with him."

Presently, Ian could see the lights on the cop car flashing up the street, and he could see that Vickie had pulled over a navy blue Buick. Ian thought that: "This is probably the Bishop." Ian took off on a run to insert himself into the fray, if it was the Bishop.

Ian approached the Buick, so that he could get a closer look, and he could now see that the driver was a priest.

Vickie yelled, "Another stinking priest. I hate priests, what are you doing here?"

The driver of the Buick said, "My dear constable, I am here to visit St. Jerome's church for this evening's vigil Mass."

Vickie was now feeling a little more bold, then grunted to her victim, "Driver's license and proof of insurance, sir, if you please."

The driver handed the requested documents to Vickie, and she read that the driver was: Joseph Sullivan of Evart, Michigan.

Vickie said, "I have heard of you, who are you, really?"

"If you must know, constable, I am the Bishop over this area of Michigan," the priest replied.

"Great flying toads!" yelled Vickie, "Not the chief holy Joe? This will not go over well with the powers that be here in Antrim Junction. Well, Father, I am issuing a ticket to you for going two miles per hour over the limit. You will have to take the ticket up with our own beloved Judge Abner Stewart."

Vickie handed the documents back to Bishop Sullivan and left abruptly.

Ian walked up to the car, and said, "I am truly sorry, Reverend Bishop. Vickie's welcome was not what I would want for you. I'm Ian MacGregor and I came down from the caretaker's house to watch for your arrival. I'm one of the few people who know that you were to be here at Mass today. May I welcome you personally, and on behalf of Father Joe Williams and Father William MacKenzie.

Bishop Sullivan was smiling, and said, "Thank you so much, Ian. I'm pleased to make your acquaintance. I believe that I should drive to the rectory at about 5 under since she hates priests. I do not want to earn another citation."

Ian wanted to assure Bishop Sullivan that he is, indeed welcome, and he said, "I'll see you at Mass, and welcome, it's a pleasure to have you here."

Bishop Sullivan replied, "Thanks, Ian, until later."

The Bishop nodded, and slowly drove his car away towards the priests residence next to St. Jerome's church.

It was getting time for Mass, and Ian reminded his father and Eric about the need to get to the church. It was important to Ian that both of them would attend this Mass. He knew that Bishop Sullivan would be presiding, and that most people would be surprised at his presence in their church. He wanted his family to be a part of the celebration.

On the way to the church, Ian said, "Father, I'm getting well settled here, and I have been helping Father Bill in regards to breaking up the illegal numbers racket here in town. Remember, that you suggested that we could become allies in this effort?"

Andrew was smiling, and said, "Ian, I am pleased that this first effort has had such a dramatic affect on the people here. Many,

many more smiles are seen while walking downtown. A sight that I personally like seeing."

Ian's smile broadened. He liked hearing his father talk like this and he said, "Thanks, father, you're in for a surprise as soon as Mass begins."

After sitting in their accustomed pews, about half way up the aisle, the MacGregors were ready for Mass. In just a few minutes the bells rang. These bells, in older buildings are used to signal that the Mass procession is about to begin and that all should stand while the priests enter the church. Upon hearing the bells everyone did stand and turned to see Bishop Sullivan coming in to preside at the celebration. Many gasps were heard among the people. The good Bishop was enjoying the surprise element. Many of the people were pleased that their Bishop was actually here in their church and presiding at the Mass. A lot of old timers believe that the Shepherd of the Diocese should be present in the local church at least once every other year.

Mass was getting under way when a disturbance was heard in the back of the church. To many in attendance, the appearance of Bud Hardwicke at the Mass was amazing. Bud, however, chose to sit in the very back pew. Some of his bettors were suddenly uneasy at his presence.

Mass went along as is customary, ending with announcements. Father Bill made the announcement that the drawing for the parish raffle would take place in the high school gym at 7PM today.

# Chapter 19

## *"The First Raffle"*

After Mass there was little time to waste before the drawing for the parish raffle. Folks were packing into the gym. It seemed that about 400 people were in there. Bishop Sullivan was likewise in attendance.

Precisely ten minutes late, the event was called to order by Father Bill. As he was reviewing the rules of the raffle and the requirements of being 18 years of age or older to participate, a small ruckus was being heard as Bud Hardwicke entered the gym. Bud was accompanied by his chauffeur. A hush was felt as Bud moved about looking the crowd over. He was trying to determine which participants were regular bettors of his, and who, were considered deserters of the ship for this week.

Once Bud found a place to sit, Father Bill was ready to continue, saying, "OK folks, we will draw the second prize first. We have asked Bishop Sullivan if he would be so kind as to draw the winners for us tonight."

The good Bishop came forward and drew the first of the winners, he called out the number, "24978".

Father Bill read the number again while looking about the crowd for the winner. Presently, there was a voice in the back saying, "It's me, it's me!!"

The crowd looked about for the face that went with that excited voice. Soon, a small man came forward with his ticket. After the winner had showed his ticket to Bishop Sullivan, and to Father Bill, it was determined that he had won the $100 gift card for grocery shopping. Bishop Sullivan was getting with the excitement of the moment.

Bishop Sullivan asked the winner, "What is your name, sir?"

The winner answered, "I am Lee Kelley from Antrim Junction. I am a life long resident here."

Father Bill handed the prize to Lee, and directed him to take his place on the stage in a special seating area set aside for the winners.

Next was the drawing for the first prize winner who would receive $500 in cash. Many people were excited that one of them would walk away with the cash. Bishop Sullivan stepped up and drew the winning ticket. The noise in the gym suddenly stopped. All were waiting for the Bishop to call out the winning number.

Bishop Sullivan spoke up and called out, "27348".

The folks that were present began to look about for the winner after they personally determined that they had not won. Soon, an older woman came forward sporting a grin. She looked as though she could hardly believe that she had won. The winner approached Bishop Sullivan with her ticket.

"My name is Molly MacDuff," she told the Bishop.

Father Bill was delighted to see that Molly had won the cash. He knew that Molly was one of Bud's victims. This $500 prize would definitely help her out at home. Helping out with food and a payment or two. Bill looked over at Bud Hardwicke and noticed that he was not having a good time. He was not sharing in the joy that Molly was indulging in. A definite air of discomfort had come over Bud Hardwicke. He was looking to determine who would receive some of his extra special offers during the next week. The rest of the winners were selected and another second prize of $100 gift card for grocery shopping and then there were three third prizes of ten tickets for the next parish raffle, just two weeks away.

As the crowd began to leave, it did not seem that anyone was disappointed at the results, except that is for Bud Hardwicke. The parish folks were pleased especially at the news that this raffle had brought in $4,270 for the grade school athletic fund. This meant that the grade school kids would have the opportunity to play baseball and soccer this summer. The parents would not have to pay any fees for summer sports, and the money is already in the bank.

Ian approached Father Bill, and said, "Gosh, Bill, I didn't realize what a dramatic impact that the results of this raffle would have on this town's folks. These people are talking to each other and they are enjoying themselves. They're seeing people that they have not seen for a long time. They're even talking with these same folks. It's so cool. The gathering at the gym was a fine event, even though only six people won a prize. The people of St. Jerome's were proud of their first effort."

Bill smiled, and added, "Ian, you're right. I couldn't be happier with the results myself. Even Bishop Sullivan was pleased to see so many people participate. I'm also delighted that Molly got the $500 prize. It'll help improve her lot in life. Her husband's paycheck is secure for this week."

Bill continued, "Ian, I understand that Vickie hassled Bishop Sullivan at her usual spot. He has to see Judge Stewart regarding going 2 miles per hour over the limit. I'm sure that the Bishop's staff will handle it. Father Lewis is quite a capable secretary for the Bishop."

"Well, Bill," Ian began, "I personally apologized to Bishop Sullivan for Vickie's conduct in writing such a petty ticket. I was just a nano second late in trying to divert Vickie from her intended hassle for another "stinking holy Joe". Vickie left the scene abruptly after delivering the ticket to Bishop Sullivan."

It seemed that the happy people of St. Jerome's kept milling about outside the gym after the drawing. They were sharing their new found happiness with each other.

In the parking lot was a disgruntled Bud Hardwicke who was the only unhappy person in Antrim Junction. Bud has estimated his losses to this week's traffic at about $7,000. He is angry, and yet he can't do anything about it.

While Father Bill and Ian were talking, they noticed that Bart Hardwicke was approaching. Bart said, "You two think that you are the victors. This time, maybe, but you don't understand how determined my granddad can be. I'll see you on Monday, skirt boy!"

Bill snickered, "Skirt boy? What is that all about?"

Ian was grinning, and said, "That's what he calls me when I wear my kilt to school. He's told me that his fee for allowing me to wear it is $1 per day. I almost planted a fist in his face over the issue, but I was able to restrain myself. So, I have increased the number of days per month that I wear my kilt above the two heritage Fridays that are scheduled."

Bill was amused at such petty picking on Bart's part and said, "Well, Ian, try to keep it down but don't let up on him. I can tell that you are getting to him, and it's funny to see his assorted reactions."

A few more minutes went by before Ian noticed that his father and Eric were leaving. Ian said to Bill, "I've gotta go, see you later."

Ian hustled to catch up with his family. Andrew was all smiles as his youngest son came up to them. He said, "Ian, I don't have the words to say to you about what a wonderful event this has been for all of us here. It is, as you have said, at last a feeling like we are at home. These folks here are excited about being together and creating a success. It will be nice to see the youngsters at play. That is organized play, and to see the parents mingling at the games and enjoying themselves and each other's company."

# Chapter 20

# "New Ideas"

Father Bill was sure that it was time to up the ante on Bud Hardwicke. It was two weeks before the next parish raffle. Ian was coming toward the picnic grove to meet with Father Bill. After a wonderful weekend, the two of them were still smiling about their first slam dunk.

Ian spoke first, "Well, Bill, it's obvious that we must do something this week before promoting the next parish raffle."

Father Bill replied, "Yes, Ian, I have been thinking about what can be done. I keep coming back to some sort of prank on Vickie and Madame. The sort that will cause embarrassment to each of them."

Ian grinned, and said, "Yes, the two perfect targets. Considering size alone, you can't miss them. Do you suppose that, somehow, we can get a hold of some of Madame's phone numbers?"

Bill thought for a moment, and said, "Well, Henry Horton owns the telephone company and he doesn't like Madame very much. Maybe he'll help out by furnishing a few of the numbers, or maybe, we can ask Eustis McKay if he knows them."

"McKay," Ian asked, "Who is that?"

Bill replied, "Eustis is an Irishman, who also is the only installer for the Horton Phone Company. If anyone would know her numbers, he would. I'm sure of that because he doesn't like making service calls to her macabre mansion. He says that she is the ultimate pest. Every little burp heard on a phone line, she calls him. After all, there is power in them ten lines."

Bill continued, "I'll visit Mr. Horton tomorrow afternoon. I'll see if we can have an ally in him. He's a prime occupant of Madame's crap list."

Ian said, "OK, let's start there and let's meet again on Wednesday afternoon, here in the grove after school."

Bill said, "OK, Ian, until then. See you."

Bill got up and walked toward the St. Jerome campus. He was in no hurry to get home and was walking at a leisurely pace. He felt a presence coming up behind him. Turning around, he saw Vickie's cop car keeping pace with him. He remembered that she did the same thing to Ian recently. So, from Ian's example, Bill slowed his pace so that Vickie soon came up beside him.

Bill turned toward Vickie, and said, "Well, Vickie, what is it now?"

With a snide sound to her voice, Vickie said, "You should go home, holy Joe. You are infecting this town with goodness, and we can't have that. We have not had two priests in town for years, and we would prefer if both of you would leave. But, I know that you won't go willingly."

Bill smiled, and said, "Vickie, our lives as priests involve commitment and compassion. Father Joe and myself gave our vows to our Bishop that we would be obedient to him and to his successors. Father Joe has suffered a stifled life here at the hands of you people. I have compassion for him. Bud Hardwicke will ultimately be defeated and after bringing this about, this town will receive a new birth of freedom, where the local residents can walk through town and not be afraid about not betting on numbers. They will at last be free from hassle about one thing or another."

Bill continued, "Vickie, I hope that you will consider what an impending demise of the Hardwicke regime will mean to you. When a really legal Chief of Police is hired here, will you still have a job? Will you command much respect with the town's people if you do keep your job, with everyone knowing what part you played in the numbers racket? These are only a few of the things that you must consider, Vickie. It could be curtains for you soon. If an undercover State Police Officer comes into Antrim Junction will you pull him over and hassle him like you did to Bishop Sullivan? These illegal numbers are of prime importance to law enforcement. In some cities, folks are getting killed for a lot less than refusing to bet on numbers. The biggest city in this state is a center of all sorts of vices at one time or another. With crime and vices being prevalent, including random murders, it is no wonder people are moving away from that city."

Vickie was sort of choking on the things that Father Bill was saying to her. She said, "Well, padre, I didn't come here to get a sermon from you, I just meant to encourage you to go home and get off the streets. Mr. Hardwicke is very irate with you and the MacGregor kid. No telling what he will do. It would be safer for the two of you to just go home and stay there."

"Thank you, Vickie," Bill began again, "But I will not hide from you like Father Joe has had to do. I will be out in the open, and I am not afraid of you, Bud, Madame, the chauffeur, or Bart, and on and on, just not. Vickie, I do need to inform you that the people of Antrim Junction are entitled to peace and quiet and a life free from any form of oppression, even if it is in the form of illegal numbers.

Bud Hardwicke and Madame are riding for a fall, and it can't come too soon."

Vickie, in a terse manner, said, "As you say, padre." Vickie abruptly drove away leaving much dust airborne.

This turn of events left Father Bill with a big grin on his face. He was certain that his presentation had given Vickie much to think about. His intention was to divide and conquer just as Ian was doing with Bart.

# Chapter 21

# "A New Ally"

Tuesday morning started out with a Mass at 8:30AM, during which Father Bill was praying for help in defeating the numbers racket. Looking up, he noticed that there were more people at the morning Mass than usual. A daily offering of the Mass is considered by some as a required start for the day. His training taught him to cherish the Mass and the daily sharing of the Eucharist, which means thanksgiving.

After Mass, Bill was talking with some of the folks in attendance. He was finding out that these people were the front leaders in feeling a bit more free in Antrim Junction. An older man who was using a cane spoke to Father Bill. He said, "Father, it is refreshing that some new free feelings are being had here at St. Jerome's. Even my old bones are feeling better at the prospect. Welcome home Bill."

Bill was taken aback at hearing this, and said, "Sir, I am pleased to hear you say this. I am a young priest and I have energy to spare. I am planning a concerted effort to bring about an end to the numbers. If we are successful, the good feelings will continue."

The old man smiled, and said, "My name is Emmett MacAllister. I am a life long resident here. It's my home and I said welcome home because I want you to feel like you're at home with us. We encourage your efforts to thumb down the Hardwickes and their numbers racket."

Bill was now grinning, and said, "Emmett, I do feel welcome, hearing it from you. The Bishop sent me here as a challenge. He wanted me to use my fresh training to the fullest extent and to help Father Joe feel better here. I plan to do just that."

Emmett smiled, and said, "Father you are home. It is my prayer that Joe will feel that way soon. If you could, please try to get him to walk about town with you. Let him see that there are faithful ones out here. We love him."

Bill excused himself. It was time to go to breakfast with Father Joe. When Bill entered the dining room, he saw that Joe was already there working on his morning crossword puzzle.

Bill said, "Good morning, Joe."

Joe smiled widely and said, "A good morning to you sir. Did Mass go well this morning?"

"Yes, as a matter of fact, it did," said Bill, "There were lots of people in attendance. I have not seen this many people at daily Mass since I have been here. I talked with Emmett MacAllistor after Mass. He made me feel quite at home here. He has great respect for you too."

Joe replied, "Emmett was at mass? It seems that I can't recall the last time that he came to a daily service. I'm pleased. On another note, Madame called this morning, and using street language, she is cranked. She all but threatened bodily damage to us if we hold the next parish raffle on schedule. The Hardwickes are particularly going after revenge toward you and Ian MacGregor. What do you think, Bill?"

Bill was not surprised in the slightest, and said, "I expected some sort of retort directed to you. With all due respect, Joe, they have stifled St. Jerome's for years. They feel that they have you just where they want you. So, therefore, they can call and threaten you, and that will have their desired affect on me. It was just last evening, as I walked home from the picnic grove, that I was in receipt of hassle number 37C from Vickie. She said to me: "Go home, holy Joe". I turned the tables on her, as I have learned to do from Ian, and said several things that could befall her if the Hardwickes are brought down. She could be out of a job, since, as you remember, Dudley Hardwicke is the present Chief of Police. When the Hardwickes go down, so goes the Chief."

Joe was smiling as he began to cover his toast with boysenberry jam, and said, "Bill, I wish you well with this effort. Joe Sullivan, while he was here, took the time to chat with me. He informed me that he's concerned that you are taking on too much here. It was his intention, at first, that this assignment would be an attitude adjustment, and as it is turning out, it is just that and then some. Look at the increase in Mass attendance here, just today. Even Bud Hardwicke was at Mass when the Bishop presided."

Bill was almost done with his food, and said, "I am pleased at the warm welcomes that the folks here keep saying to me. I will do my best to keep them coming in."

After breakfast, Bill decided to walk over to the Horton Phone Company. It was located one block farther north on Main Street past Elm, at the corner of Maple Street. Upon arrival, Bill discovered that it was a single story building of aged red brick with a slanting roof from front to back. Large black phone cables entered the building from the Maple Street side, from old fragile poles. Bill found the entrance. Posted on the door was a sign that indicated that the business hours were from 9AM to 12:30PM. Bill noted that he was in time. He entered the building and heard the bell that rang upon being hit with the door.

Soon, a little man came out. He was no more than five feet tall, and for appearances sake, he looked like he had a part in a W.C. Fields movie. He had jet black hair, a bushy moustache, wore black glasses, and of course he was smoking a stogie. One luxury that Henry Horton had over Bishop Sullivan was that he had the money to buy a better quality cigar. The smoke from Henry's cigar was not nearly as objectionable as that generated by the good Bishop.

The man spoke to Father Bill, "May I help you sir?"

Bill replied, "Yes sir, I hope that you can. I'm Father Bill MacKenzie from St. Jerome's parish. As you know, I have taken up the cross of trying to break the choke hold that the Hardwickes have on this town. It has been a fruitful first effort to have the raffle last week."

Henry spoke up, "Where would I fit into your plan to stifle these guys?"

Bill began again, "Well, Mr. Horton, we would like to begin a telephone assault on Madame, in an effort to confuse their operation. By doing so, we hope to chase away even more customers. The numbers racket is only going to make the dollars that Bud wants if he keeps up the betting traffic. He has already upped the prize amounts that he pays over the State Lottery payouts to $200 extra. He can't keep this up with the presence of a legal raffle that we are licensed for. What I came down here for, is, well, Mr. Horton, we need some of her phone numbers."

Henry smiled, "That's all? Well, her ten lines are unlisted except in my master log, which I will inadvertently leave on the counter for a few minutes. I can't always keep folks from looking through it if I can't see them doing it. Let me remind you that Madame is an affliction to running the phone company. The ten lines, call directors, making two hundred calls a day, making a pest of herself with my installer Eustis are the points of concern and my problems with her. Eustis has lots of real work to do rather than to placate that over stuffed blob. I call her at least three times a week and I ask her to please limit her calls so that some other people, who also pay for their service, can get a dial tone for once. If you will excuse me for a few minutes, I will be right back."

Bill realized that Henry was helping, but he also noted that he had to help himself to her numbers from the inadvertantly exposed log book that was left open to Madame's page, and so marked. After Bill had the numbers written down, he closed the book. When Henry heard the book being closed, he returned to the front counter.

Henry said, "Well, Father, I welcome some peace coming over us here in Antrim Junction. If Madame were trimmed back to normalcy, maybe the gossip mill will never need another grease job. If you should ever get those phone numbers, give her the business."

Henry was grinning from ear to ear. He knew full well that Bill had written down all the numbers from the log book.

Henry began again, "Can I offer some help for the next raffle? I will offer for third prizes a $40 gift certificate toward their phone bills. The raffle tickets for the next raffle can move back to fourth prizes."

Bill was pleased to hear Henry talk like this. He was, after all, the first local businessman who has offered to participate in the prizes.

Bill said, "Yes, Mr. Horton, please do so. There should be two of them."

Henry was beaming, "Yes, sir, it's a done deal. And, as far as Madame goes, sock it to her and give a little to Vickie as well. She is such a pest, and keep in mind, Vickie has never done any real police work. She only stops people at the speed limit sign. Which is a sign that one can hardly see. Then she furnishes hassle and petty cheap shot tickets. She could direct her immenseness toward things that are clearly awry in town and leave regular folks alone."

Father Bill was pleased. Here was a new ally. Bill knew that Ian would be pleased as well.

Bill said, "Thank you, Mr. Horton, your inadvertent help is appreciated, and your prize offer is very welcomed. I'll see you soon."

After Bill left the phone company office, he walked south on Main Street toward the now famous Elm Street, the home of Madame Blimpneflah. Just to Bill's left he could see the yellow house. He mused that there will be confusion there very soon, and the next peg in the row was now coming into view. This is Bart Hardwicke. Bart was leading an entourage of dutiful ill-reputes as they went about looking important to no one but themselves and delivering hassle to a few folks. These folks were not receptive to Bart's interference.

Bill walked up to Bart, and said, "Bart, imagine seeing you out in broad daylight. I thought that when the sun came up, it affected the folks on the dark side."

Bart was sensing an overt encounter with the good padre. Bart said, "Well, Bill, are you going about doing good in an effort to erase my gains?"

Bill replied, "I just wanted to ask you if you would consider helping us out at the high school this weekend. We are going through our baseball and soccer equipment. We need to sort out things that need replacing."

Bart's sarcastic bravado was growing, and he said, "Bill, I

couldn't care less about that sports stuff. Those kids can use that old equipment for all I care. Your sports leaders just think that they're hot stuff since they got a large infusion of Hardwicke cash into the athletic fund."

Bill quickly answered, "On the contrary, Bart, they don't just think that they are hot stuff, they know it. Their intention is to pull off a startlingly successful season for the elementary kids. The parent interest is already keen. It will be successful. We are adopting an everyone plays format."

Bart said, "Well, lah dee dah."

Bill wanted to beat Bart to the punch, and said, "Bart, you are dismissed."

## Chapter 22

# "Action At The Speed Trap"

Thursday evening had arrived. Father Bill was having a clandestine meeting of sorts with some of the victims of the illegal numbers. Some of the husbands came with their wives. Mostly it was the wives of the chronic bettors that were in attendance.

Bill said, "Folks, this is where we have to stick together in our common effort to bring down the numbers racket in Antrim Junction. We'll begin a barrage of confusing communications tomorrow afternoon. While this barrage is underway, the men will gather at Main and Elm Streets. They'll be there to interfere with the pick up of the betting slips and the money transfer to the chauffeur."

"The scenario will begin about 5PM with the ladies calling all ten of Madame's phone lines at the same time. This will tie her up for better than an hour. It's up to you, ladies, as to how outrageous you can get with Madame. Remember to keep her busy. If she hangs up on you, call her right back. Remember to use star 67 on your phone so her caller ID will not show who's calling. In addition to calling Madame, you will also have to keep calling Bart Hardwicke's cell phone, tying him up also. Plus someone needs to be selected to call Vickie to their house for some sort of a cat up in a tree emergency."

"At about 5:30PM, the men will begin to gather at Main and Elm. When the limo is sighted, we'll gather around the courier and cause such confusion with yelling and arguments that the chauffeur will have to get out of the car to try to gather the money and the bet slips."

The temperament of the crowd was one of excitement.

One of the ladies spoke up, and said, "Father Bill, I have always wanted to insult Madame Blimpneflah but I did not have the nerve to do so. This gives me a chance to annoy her to the nth degree. I will keep her phone numbers on record if they are ever needed again."

Bill continued, "We are also going to conduct a hassle of Madame and Vickie earlier in the day. If you go past the ugly yellow house on Elm Street in the early part of the morning, look for some sign that will be posted on her picket fence. Some of the kids will picket Vickie at the speed trap, and I guarantee you that she will be ticked off before the time of the sting."

"Ian MacGregor is coordinating that effort with some of the students from St. Jerome's High School. He's determined to see that our town will be as good a home as was his fatherland. His fatherland was dearly loved by himself. He is slowly becoming a Michigan Scot."

"It's time to break into groups so that each group will focus on their part in this event. Let's do some fine tuning for each of our roles."

The evening ended about a half hour later with all of the parties ready with their parts. Ian was to meet with Father Bill after the group left.

Ian said, "Bill, you have gotten all of these people excited about being part of bringing peace to their town. It's so cool."

Bill began his presentation to Ian, "Ian, in the morning, your group will be down at the speed trap, and they will carry these signs. The first two will have to be south of the City Limit sign at half block intervals. The rest of the picket signs will be carried right at the sign location. You are familiar with the location of the first stop in town that Andrew went through."

Ian said, "Yes, I won't forget that for some time to come. Bill, I just love these signs. Who made these for you?"

Bill, kind of winking, said, "Well, Father Joe and our secretary made the signs. Do you like the first two? "Speed trap up ahead" and "Almost to the speed trap!" Then here are the ones that will be held up at the speed trap: "Vickie on Rye", "Cochise can hide behind Vickie", "We smell a rat" and, I like this one, "The rat is in the cop car"."

Ian was laughing at this point, and he managed to say, "Bill, this is beyond cool. These signs will enrage the dirigible cop. She might react like a bull in a china shop and aimlessly be bumping into people all around."

Bill turned his demeanor to the serious side, and said, "Ian, this is serious stuff. We're sticking our collective necks out a long, long way here. We could get hurt. So let's not lose sight of the mission at hand. If we can get the chauffeur and the courier arrested, then Bud will have to sit up and take notice that he will be next."

The next morning, before school, Ian and his friends were gathered at the City Limit sign at the south edge of Antrim Junction. The kids were spaced at half block intervals with the speed trap signs. Ian and the others were stationed at the speed trap itself. Presently, here comes the cop car going north from the IGA store 1 block south. Vickie probably stopped there to get her caffeine booster refilled. Viewing the cop car coming toward him, Ian noticed that she was doing a small amount of swerving while trying to read the signs.

Ian sad to his friends, "Look out, here she comes. She's already ticked!"

Vickie was almost out of control when she saw the sign that said: "Vickie on rye". She stopped the cop car and got out. She was totally red faced.

Vickie yelled at the kids, "I ought to run all of you in for this! You cannot create a disturbance here!"

Ian spoke up, "But, Vickie, we are not disturbing anyone. It is you that is creating a disturbance. It may even be classed as disturbing the peace or being disorderly."

"Shut up, MacGregor," yelled an irate Vickie.

"Yes, your royal fatness." Ian managed to say amid much snickering. "You know, Vickie, you're not making a good impression on school age kids, who are just here expressing their freedom of speech, which as you know, is a constitutionally guaranteed freedom."

Vickie blurted back, "I do not need to come down here to get insulted."

Ian snapped at her, "Then where do you want to be insulted?"

Vickie was getting more steamed as the minutes went by. She said, "Doesn't school start at 8:30? I think that you kids need to get up to St. Jerome's High School, like pronto!"

Ian said, "We will consider it. It is our right to be here, and it is not your right to hassle us for expressing ours."

After the kids left for school, for which they were in time, Vickie sat in the cop car to reflect on the events that had just transpired. She picked up her cell phone to call Madame. Madame answered quickly. Vickie said, "Madame, I have just encountered a gang of kids picketing at the speed limit sign. Two of them warned drivers of a speed trap up ahead, but four others were personally offensive to me."

Madame was just mildly amused. She had just noticed a sign in front of her house. Thinking that she should check it out, she informed Vickie that she would call her back, as something was happening there.

Madame waddled out to the mailbox. When she opened the gate, she saw a poster that read, "Madame Blimpneflah is a big old dork!" Instantly, Madame was in a rage. Slamming her gate behind, she went back into her house. Madame picked up the hot line and called Vickie back.

Madame said, "Vickie, get over here at once. You have to see that I have been maligned at my own home and the neighbors are laughing at me!"

Vickie said, "Right away, Madame." The call ended.

Vickie must have been only a few blocks away when she was called to attend to this earth shaking event. When the cop car turned east on Elm Street, a squawking of tires could be heard. Less than a minute had gone by since Madame called. As Vickie pulled up to the yellow house, Madame was coming back out to the sidewalk.

Madame began, "Vickie, I have never been dealt like this before. What are you going to do about it?"

Vickie replied, "What should I do about it? Did you see anyone put this poster here? Did you realize that anyone would want to do such a thing?"

Madame was feeling exasperated, and she continued, "Vickie, I have been maligned by someone who is unknown to me at this time. I can't imagine who would stoop this low."

Vickie added, "Well, just this morning, I was picketed by some high school kids with a sign that said "Vickie on Rye", "Cochise

Can Hide Behind Vickie". and "The Rat is in the Cop Car". This took place at the city limit sign. The MacGregor kid was the ring leader.

Madame was instantly ticked off, and said, "MacGregor must have done this on his way to the speed trap location. I told that kid last week that he and the padre were walking a thin line here for meddling in our enterprises."

Vickie added, "Madame, you didn't see him and you can't prove that he did it either. We will just have to be more observant in the future."

Madame snatched the sign, ripped it up, and took the pieces inside with her. The unceremonious departure of Madame was memorable.

## Chapter 23

# "The Sting"

With the success of the morning campaign, the kids attended school in a very good mood, indeed. No one was tardy, and at noon, lunch was going well, with Bart keeping his distance.

When Ian took his place at the lunch table, Bart came over and sat down.

Bart said, "Ian, just a word of warning. You and the padre have enraged the establishment here, and now war has been declared. You two can't get away with this. We will stop you."

Ian suddenly became terse, and said, "Bart, you are quite right, we WILL stop you. You will have to pay for your crimes. You know full well that the sin of complacency will get to you soon. Bud Hardwicke is an old man who needs to stop his stuff and leave people alone so that he can enjoy his declining years. True, he will have to earn his income honestly, but don't we all?"

Bart was showing discomfort at this line of thought, and said, "Ian, I think that you talk much braver than you are. Granddad will prevail. When we do, life will be even tighter than it has been."

Ian was wanting to finish his meal, and said, "Whatever you say, Bart. The good will prevail, and the crime will be squashed. If you want to talk about sports, OK, enough talk about Bud's ultimate demise."

Bart stood up, and said, "I warn you, MacGregor, you will pay the consequences." He walked away.

Ian knew what would take place in the afternoon. As the plan was to picket Madame's house during the hassle time. Ian knew that he could see up the street to where the sting would be taking place. Such knowledge gave him pleasure to be in the know. After school, Ian went directly to fetch his picket sign which was specifically planned for Madame's house. Ian went to the dining room of the caretaker's house for a short break. Soon, Andrew came into the room.

Andrew said, "Ian, what is going on today? There seems to be much upheaval in town."

Ian began, "Well, father, we staged a picket line at the speed trap this morning so that Vickie would get herself disheveled, and that in turn would put Madame in the first throes of complete confusion. This will continue in the next hour. Don't worry, father, there will be State Police officers present when the big event happens, between 5PM and 6PM. Remember, it was at your suggestion that the State Police troopers would be consulted. We are making substantial headway at breaking the grip that the Hardwickes have on this town."

Andrew was showing concern about his youngest son, and said, "Ian, I am pleased that the good feeling that has been present since the church raffle seems to be lasting. But, my concern is that you might get hurt."

"Father," Ian said, "Yours is the same concern that Father Bill expressed to me, just yesterday. The police are in town right now, and at the appointed time, they will arrest the number courier, and Bud's chauffeur. With these guys in the can, at least temporarily, Bud may feel that he can be defeated, and may, possibly give in."

Andrew replied, "Ian, just be careful. I do not want to have to go somewhere to pick up the pieces. Now finish your snack and be on your way. I want to hear all about the event when you return."

"Aye, sir, father," Ian said quickly.

When Ian was ready, he began to walk south along the service drive. He was carrying his latest insult placard for Madame Blimpneflah. When he reached Elm Street, he looked to his right to see if any crowd was visible yet. Checking his watch, he knew that he needed to be in his place in five minutes. In the same few minutes, Madame's call director will look like a Las Vegas style light display. She will be receiving ten calls at once. At the same time, Bart will be tied up with a frivolous call. Vickie will also be busy as she will be summoned to a resident assist call.

Ian walked up to the yellow house and hoisted his sign up for all to see: "Madame is an overweight doakaramus". Ian could see a bit inside to notice that the bright light is on by Madame's phone center. Madame could be seen from the street. She was bound to notice his presence outside of her window. Ian began to wave the sign back and forth in the direction of the window where she is talking on the telephone.

Ian could sense that she has many lines in action at this time. There is a look of disgust on her face. Ian could see that Madame is punching the line button selectors and then hanging up on callers. She seems to be progressively irate with the callers.

Looking up toward Main Street, Ian could see the courier on the far corner. There was no one else in sight. Soon, a few walkers began to appear from all directions. A few more minutes went by and it was the courier who made the first move by crossing the street. This placed the courier on the east side of Main Street, just west of Madame's house. Here he took up his place to wait for the black limo. He was standing in this place just as he was the first time that Ian had seen him there.

While Ian was watching the sting scene, he didn't notice that Madame had seen him outside of her house. Suddenly, Madame burst through the front door and was heading toward Ian with a baseball bat in hand. Madame yelled, "MacGregor, hit the road this instant!"

Ian reacted quickly, and turned the sign so that Madame could directly see it, and just as quickly, she came unglued as she read the message. At the same time a disturbance was underway at the corner of Main and Elm. Both Ian and Madame turned to look toward the event. In quick succession, there was a scuffle with a group of men, the courier, and the chauffeur. This was followed by the flashing lights from the State Police cars which were coming in from four directions. Soon, Vickie came west on Elm Street from the service drive in her cop car. Vickie's car came to a halt in front of Madame's house.

Vickie said, "What is going on here?"

Madame replied, "I reckon that MacGregor knows all about it. You can rest assured that it is another assault on our enterprises."

Vickie spoke up, and said, "I'll go down there to see what is going down."

Ian added, "I'll see you two rotund ones later!"

Ian ran off toward the fracas. When he got to the corner, Ian could see that the courier and the chauffeur were locked in the back seat of the State Police squad car. Vickie is seeming to be a third wheel in the chat about the event as the troopers were making notes about what had happened. The rest of the people that are milling about are sporting wide grins, and they seem to be happy with themselves.

Later on in the evening, Ian and Father Bill were together in the picnic grove. Bill said, "Ian, the police have reported that the bags contained over four thousand dollars and more than two thousand bet slips. Remember that this pick up point at Main and Elm is only one of four such points. So, if you expand the math, you come up with about $16,000 to $20,000 per week. From far and wide in this area, that is a lot of money each week going to the Hardwickes. What we have done is taken away only one fourth of their take this week. Next week, our own parish raffle will take even more from their till."

Ian replied, "Bill, we have made such a shamble of their crime coordination, that the confusion at the pick up site went perfectly well. It happened with such speed that even Madame was amazed. As I was picketing her house at the time that it all went down."

Bill continued, "Ian, you are right, everything went off like clockwork. Vickie is one scrambled up cop at this point. She can't seem to figure out what happened, and to the State Police people, she is just a horrible joke foisted on the people here. The State Police will not let her in on anything because of the crime family ties that are in town."

"Dudley is going to be hard pressed to explain her to the Post Commander. He will want to pursue all aspects of the numbers crime that all of them have been a party to thus far. The commander will, no doubt, be in town in the next few days as their investigation continues."

Ian replied, "Yes, Madame is quite ticked off and there's no telling what they will try to do next. We must press on to the next raffle. I understand that we have other prizes from businessmen in town who want in on the action."

Bill smiled, and replied, "Yes, there are two third prizes of $40 gift cards for telephone service, 6 third prizes for $15 of dry cleaning, and 6 third prizes of a pair of child's sneakers for the upcoming summer sports, and of course, the fourth prizes are tickets to the next parish raffle."

"It sounds so good that the local people want a part in the prizes," said Ian, "This could grow into quite a positive thing."

Bill replied, "Yes, I'm hoping so. The more the parishioners participate, the better the results will be and the greater the impact of the good that comes from it. We need to break off now and go our own ways. We are being watched. Look over there, the cop car is in view."

The two of them got up and left the picnic grove. Ian went north along the service drive heading to the caretaker's house. Father Bill went south toward the St. Jerome rectory.

# Chapter 24

# "The Investigation Begins"

T he next morning, being Saturday, Ian was wondering just what
the day would bring. It was warming up quite nicely outside,
and spring had a firm grip on northern Michigan. The blessings of
high pressure brought crystal clear blue skies to Antrim Junction.
Also there was 60 degree temperatures. Ian decided that a leisurely
walk was in order.

After breakfast, Ian left the caretaker's house and proceeded
south on the service drive toward St. Jerome's church. As he approached the church, he could see Father Bill on the veranda talking
with some of the folks who had attended the morning Mass. Ian
decided that this was one of Bill's favorite events. It put him into
contact with the people who were the strongest in their faith.

Ian waved to Bill and continued on his walk toward the speed
trap. Ian, being a little curious, decided to walk the one block south
to the IGA store to see what Vickie's attraction to it is all about.

When Ian arrived at the store, he could see that Vickie's cop car
was parked out in the front parking lot. Once he entered the building, he could see that Vickie was in the deli to get her coffee canister
filled with her daily brew. Ian estimated that the canister held about
32 ounces of hot coffee, and being insulated, it would last at least to

mid-afternoon. Musing about why Vickie always worked 10 hours a day, Ian realized that all she did was to give out speed trap tickets.

Presently, Vickie turned about to go to her car, and she saw Ian standing there sporting a whimsical grin. Vickie said, "MacGregor, what are you doing this far south?"

Ian retorted, "Vickie, I was just curious about your attraction to this deli, and why the cop car is always here in the early hours. What if some crime would go down! You couldn't handle it, and probably wouldn't."

Vickie was beginning to get steamed at Ian, she said, "MacGregor, watch your mouth. I could run you in."

Ian smirked, and said, "Run me in where? There is no jail here. There is no Chief of Police that is worth a mound of dust. Just what could you do?"

An irate Vickie blurted, "Watch out brat, I'm watching you!!"

Vickie stormed out of the IGA and left amid much noise. Outside there was a lot of dust airborne having been kicked up by the rapid departure of Vickie's cop car.

Ian purchased a pop and left the IGA. He began to walk north toward the speed trap. He could probably antagonize Vickie some more up there. This seemed to be great sport for Ian.

At the speed trap, Ian could see that Vickie had pulled over a car. He was curious and approached the scene so that he could take in more of the action. Ian began to grin when he realized that the driver was the State Police investigator, and he was in uniform, and he was driving an unmarked car. The officer was visibly irate.

The State Trooper said, "What do you think that you're doing? Can't you see who you are dealing with?"

Vickie replied, "Sir, you were doing 3 miles per hour over the limit and you deserved to be pulled over. In an unmarked car, an officer could not possibly tell that you are a police officer."

The trooper was getting louder, and said, "Vickie, if you would be so kind as to accompany me to your station, I will interrogate Chief Dudley Hardwicke so that I can determine the validity of what you seem to habitually do here at this sign. It seems, as has been reported, that you have been picketed recently, and that the information contained on the signs said, "Speed Trap Up Ahead", and "Almost to the speed trap". Is this correct?"

Vickie gulped, and replied, "Yes, sir, it is completely correct. If you will follow my car, I will take you to the station."

Ian watched as the two cop cars went north on Main Street. The Police operation was housed in a combination building on Main Street. This building also contained the City Hall offices and in the rear was a small local fire department. The fire department area was under construction to facilitate newly enacted rules that require drive through garages for fire trucks. Upon arrival, Vickie and the Sergeant investigator went inside.

Inside the station, Vickie said, "Sergeant, if you will wait here for a moment, I will fetch Chief Hardwicke."

Vickie was gone about five minutes, and when she returned, she announced, "This way, Sergeant."

The two of them walked down a short hallway and into a conference room. They were soon joined by Chief Dudley. After his entry, Dudley introduced himself and sat down.

Dudley said, "Welcome, Sergeant, how may we help you?"

Sergeant Brown began, "Well, Chief, as you know, our officers from the Kalkaska Post arrested two persons here in Antrim Junction just yesterday. I am following up with the investigation. It seems that, upon interrogation of the suspects, that the Hardwicke family is involved in the illegal numbers racket that is prevalent in this part of the county. The suspects had over four thousand dollars in their courier bags, as well as about two thousand bet slips for various events. The persons that were arrested are employees of one Mr. Bud Hardwicke. The most visible of whom is Mr. Hardwicke's chauffeur. The chauffeur is the means of transporting the swag over to the Hardwicke residence. It is there that the monies and the bet slips are sorted as to the amount of the bets and for which day and the numbers that were bet on. Further, Chief, it appears that you have the same surname as the aforementioned Bud Hardwicke. I am here to ask you where you fit into this scheme?"

Dudley was choking on the question, and began, "Well, sir, I am the Chief of Police here in Antrim Junction, Michigan. I was appointed by Mayor Richard Leslie, and confirmed by the City Council. I direct the operation of the department, with Vickie and five other officers. Your assertion of a crime hook between myself and my brother is an affront to me."

Sergeant Brown began another line of questioning, "Just what are your qualifications to have this job? What police academy did you graduate from? What management credentials do you possess?"

Dudley was visibly shaken, and said, "Sergeant Brown, my credentials are on record at the City Clerk's office, you can check there, and you can interview the Mayor if you have any other substantive questions."

Sergeant Brown began again, "Just what is Vickie's assignment? It seems to me that she operates a speed trap at the south City Limits, and according to folks that I have interviewed, not much else but sucking down coffee, and consorting with a person identified as Madame Blimpneflah."

Dudley stood up, and said, "Our interview is concluded." Dudley left the room.

Sergeant Brown said, "Well, Vickie, it seems that Dudley feels that he can't handle this right now. I suggest that you find out the answers yourself, so that when an administrative law judge comes to town, you can answer truthfully to his questions. This will expand on my investigation. He will probe the administration of this Police Department and he will determine the qualifications of the officers, including you and the Chief, and he will render a decision as to who will continue to work here."

At this point, Sergeant Brown exited the conference room, and turning, he went to locate the Mayor's office. After several tries, the way to the Mayor's office was marked with arrows, and in a few more minutes, he had located the office.

Trooper Brown entered the Mayor's ante room where the secretary worked also as a receptionist, she said, "May I help you, sir?"

Sergeant Brown said, "Yes you can. I must meet with Mayor Leslie. Here are my credentials."

The secretary looked over his documents, and said, "Just one moment, sir."

In a few minutes there appeared in the doorway a man, small in stature, and a little pudgy, who said, "Sergeant Brown, I am Richard Leslie, mayor of this berg. Please come with me."

Sergeant Brown was now in another conference room to meet with Mayor Richard Leslie. Mr. Leslie said, "How can I help you?"

Sergeant Brown began, "Mr. Mayor, as you know, a sting was held here yesterday, and two of your residents were arrested for possession of illegal number racket betting slips and a large amount of cash. These two persons were identified as employees of Mr. Bud Hardwicke. The coincidence comes into play here with the same name Hardwicke is the Chief of Police here. I am here to ask you just how Dudley Hardwicke became the Chief of Police and what were the qualifications that he possessed that persuaded the council to hire him into that position. Dudley informed me that his qualifications are on record here."

Mayor Leslie replied, "Well, sir, the name similarity seems obvious as Dudley is, in fact, Bud's brother. It would also seem likely that Bud pulls Dudley's chain. And that Bud Hardwicke runs this town. Quite true. I am the Mayor, in name only, and for the most part, I have no clue as to what goes on in the crime business. My part in the day to day operation of the City is that of supervisor, over the department heads. My signature is required on all documents of merit including paychecks. As for the operation of the numbers, Bud is the guy. I am a titular person with regards the Police Department. Let me bring in Dudley's file."

A gesture was made to the secretary and shortly she brought in the requested file. As files go, it did not seem to be very thick.

Mayor Leslie said, "Here you go. You can see that Dudley worked previously at the Kingston Brothers Land Fill, Incorporated, and that he has a GED, and that he has no prior police training or experience of any kind whatsoever."

Sergeant Brown said, "Just as I thought. He was placed in his job to facilitate the numbers without interference. How this took place will be investigated. I will return on Monday to see you in the afternoon, and you are to be ready to comply with all the records sought in the search warrant that I will bring with me. We will get to the bottom of this."

At that Sergeant Brown stood up, and said, "Good day to you, sir." Sergeant Brown left the Mayor's conference room.

# Chapter 25

## *"Kidnapped"*

There was a flurry of telephone calls placed from the City Hall and Police complex before the Saturday hours ended at 1PM. There were calls from Dudley to Bud, from Vickie to Madame, and calls from Mayor Leslie to Bud and Madame.

Henry Horton was probably amused at seeing such a large volume of calls on a Saturday afternoon. Particular attention was drawn to the parties that were talking. The phones were holding up with the increase in traffic, but just barely.

Bud picked up his phone, and said, "Hello, who is calling?"

The caller said, "Bud, old boy, it is Dudley. We are in a peck of trouble. The State Police Investigator was just here demanding to know how I got this job and what my qualifications are. He also wants to know how I fit into the ability of your running the numbers racket here in town. I am a stuck pig. What are you going to do? I thought that this job was going to be a peach, where I could push most of the real work over on the Sergeant of the Watch."

Bud answered, "Settle down Dudley. Let me think about what will have to happen. With the chauffeur and one courier in jail, we are definitely hampered. This coming weekend is the second of the

St. Jerome's parish raffles and we could still see another sizable drop in cash. You are the Chief for now, and as such, we will need your input to bring forth a victory."

Dudley retorted, "Bud, you are woefully mistaken. They have almost gotten the whole picture in focus. They will descend upon you and the machine in force soon. He told Leslie that he will be presenting a search warrant at City Hall on Monday afternoon and you know what that means!"

Bud was now feeling lower, and said, "I understand your concern but you must look the other way when I make the next move. Keep your officers busy with trivial stuff in the meantime."

Dudley was much throttled back and said, "OK brother."

Meanwhile, Ian was heading home when he saw Father Bill up ahead at the picnic grove. He walked up to Bill and said, "Hey, what's doing?"

Bill, grimacing, said, "Ian, the police investigator has been in town all morning long. He was even a target for Vickie and one of her famous petty ticket attempts, all because he was driving an unmarked car, and, get this, he was in uniform!"

Ian was now smiling, and said, "I was there, and I saw the whole thing. When it was determined that she should back off, he invited her to lead him to the Police Station so that he could meet Chief Dudley. As you know, the Mayor's office and the Chief of Police offices are open on Saturdays until 1PM so that working folks can see them during the morning hours."

Bill added, "It must have been at this morning's office hours that the investigator informed the two of them of an intense investigation. Word has it that he will return on Monday afternoon with a City Hall search warrant. You and I must lay low during the next few days. Bud and his cronies will certainly seek revenge on us. Watch your step as you move about town and keep away from Vickie. The jobs of Vickie and Dudley are in jeopardy."

After the vigil Mass, at 5PM Saturday, Ian was walking toward the caretaker's house. He again felt a presence behind him. Looking back, Ian saw that it was Vickie in the cop car trailing behind him. Vickie now proceeded to come up directly beside Ian.

Vickie said, "MacGregor, stop where you are. Get in!"

Ian was instantly cranked, and said, "Why should I bother to listen to you? I am on my way home after all."

Vickie is getting insistant, and screeched, "Now, MacGregor, now!!"

Reluctantly, Ian got into the cop car. He said, "Where are you taking me?"

Vickie said, "Just shut up, MacGregor, and keep quietly to yourself."

Vickie turned the cop car around, and began to drive south on the service drive. She turned right onto Elm Street. Then she suddenly turned left into the driveway of the ugly yellow house. Instantly Ian knew where he was going.

Vickie got out of the cop car and opened the door for Ian. Vickie said, "Get out, MacGregor, and come with me."

Vickie led the way into the service entrance on the east side of Madame's house. Vickie yelled, "In here, MacGregor, and sit down, now!!"

Ian did as he was told. Soon, Madame entered the room and sat down at the table where Ian was seated. Madame said, "Well, we meet again. I mean to teach you some means of respect, MacGregor. Because you have no respect for our establishment and you have tried to bring us down ever since you arrived in town."

Ian asked, "Why have you two fat blobs kidnapped me anyway? This could mean a load of crap coming your way."

Madame asserted herself immediately, and said, "Shut up MacGregor, and we won't have you killed right away. Instead, I have prepared some supper for you and I will have some if you don't die from it."

Ian now realized that his predicament was dire. He understood what Father Bill was worried about. Ian had to decide to come to grips with his situation: "I have been kidnapped, and I am being held as a hostage."

As the evening wore on, Andrew MacGregor became concerned about Ian not being in the house. Andrew began looking up the service drive to the south toward the church. He could not see his son. It was now about 8PM and there is no sign of Ian. Andrew thought it would be fruitless to call the local police, since the Hardwickes controlled the police department. So, Andrew called the State Police post in Kalkaska. He reported that his son had not come home today. He told them that he feared that Ian had met with some foul play as a result of the recent sting just yesterday.

A half hour passed before the State Police were at the caretaker's house. Father Bill arrived just seconds later. The meeting was to determine the recent events, as to who saw Ian last, and where and when.

Bill said, "I had just discussed with Ian about the need to watch one's step. I was sure that Bud would seek some kind of revenge on us. It wasn't but a few hours ago, in the picnic grove. I haven't seen him since."

The Sergeant of the Watch was present as the leader of the team. The Sergeant said, "We must proceed delicately as we cannot risk any harm to Ian. We have to address each of the individuals in question, one at a time. I believe that one of them has Ian detained."

Bill asked, "Who are these suspects?"

Sergeant Smith replied, "According to my notes, furnished by Sergeant Brown, they are Vickie, Madame Blimpneflah, Dudley Hardwicke, and Richard Leslie. These four people will be checked out first. The first impression is that they are hooked together at the hips. When Bud Hardwicke moves, it results in a chain reaction to all of them."

Sergeant Smith talked briefly with each person present at the caretaker's house, and then left. He said that there will be much action in town over the next few days.

Bill lagged behind and said, "Andrew, we have to take things into our own hands. We just can't let it be that Ian is missing just like that."

Presently, there was a knock at the door, Bill went to answer it, and found that it was Elise Leslie from the school. Elise came in. She was visibly shaken and in quite a dither.

Elise said, "Father Bill, I saw Vickie pick up Ian and take him away in the cop car. There was a lot of yelling and then Ian was gone."

Bill sat down, and said, "Where do you think Ian has been taken? Here in town?"

Elise began again. Her voice was trembling, "Father, I would watch Madame's house. I would bet a dollar and a doughnut that he is being held there. If Mr. Hardwicke is seen going in there then I would say it is a sure thing that Ian is in there."

While this meeting was going on, a Hardwicke was at Madame's ugly yellow house, but it was Bart, instead. Bart went to where Ian was being kept.

Bart said, "Ian, I warned you. You're in a jam. A jam so gooey that it will be hard to get out. You're being kept here until the padre says uncle, cancels all the raffles, and leaves town. Madame will see to it that you are fed, that you have a place to sleep, and that you have access to a personal rest room. Until later, Ian, I bid you tata. Feel at home?"

With that remark, Bart left Madame's house. This left Ian alone with Madame, a thrill that he could suppress.

Bart came and went unseen by the parties at the caretaker's house. Their concern about Ian was strong. They were planning to observe Madame's house between now and Monday when the State Police will be back in full force.

Father Bill was taking Ian's disappearance rather hard. Bill said, "I just can't accept that they would take Ian as a hostage. They can't be that low. If you will excuse me, I will walk back home and eye Madame's house myself."

Bill's trip back to the rectory was lengthened by a half hour of watching Madame's house. When Bill arrived at the rectory, he was greeted by Joe Williams almost immediately.

Joe shouted, "Bill! There has been an unidentified call for you and here is the message: "We have the MacGregor kid, and we will keep him until you announce the permanent cancellation of any future parish raffles and that you will leave town. We will take care of him for at least three days. A visible reply is required.""

Joe continued, "Bill, what has happened?"

Bill began, "Well, Joe, Ian has been kidnapped. He was taken by Vickie in the cop car. Elise from our school saw Vickie take him away but she didn't see where they went. They are running scared. The State Police are closing in on them. Ian is probably being held at Madame's house on Elm Street. Tomorrow, all vigilance will be spent on watching that ugly house. If there is a sign of any of the Hardwickes there, we will call in the troopers."

Joe added, "I was afraid that Bud would take revenge on you guys. I pray that no one will get hurt. Ian is a tough kid and truly loyal besides. He deserves better, and if we prevail, he will have it.

# Chapter 26

## "Another Kidnapping"

Ian was perplexed with his situation. He was wondering what he could do to get out of here. He was getting tired and he decided to go to sleep. There was a small cot size bed in his detention room.

Ian was resting well when the light of morning broke over the horizon. Bright sunlight began to enter the room to reveal that Madame has not painted this room in many years. It appeared to be quite tattered. Ian didn't want to get up. He knew that Madame would exert her immenseness over him very soon. He decided to remain laying down until that ultimate event was to develop.

About 8:30AM, Madame was heard bumping around in the kitchen nearby. She was talking to herself, but it was not at a level that was intelligible. Ian surmised that she was rehearsing her presentation to him.

A few more minutes went by and then the dirigible burst into the room with a tray of food. A bowl of oatmeal with raisins, which was hot, a glass of milk, and some toast. A fitting normal breakfast for a young Scot.

"Get up, MacGregor, now!!" she yelled at him. "You have to eat your meal now. You have things to do this morning."

Ian was in no hurry to gulp down the breakfast. He felt that the healthy approach to eating was a deliberate one, not hurried. He intended to consume all of his meal but not to invite indigestion from eating too fast.

Ian asked Madame, "What do you fat blobs want me to do?"

Madame quickly replied, "Just wait, I will inform you when the time comes."

Ian continued to eat his oatmeal, when suddenly a commotion was heard outside near the entry way. The commotion made its way into where Ian was being held. Ian looked up to see the familiar form of Vickie. She was not alone. Ian looked closer so that he could see that the other person was Elise. Elise was putting up a lot of resistance to Vickie's effort to shove her into the room.

Ian was instantly mad and said, "Vickie, what are you doing roughing up Elise?"

Vickie made a terse response, "Shut up, MacGregor, no one spoke to you!" Vickie pushed Elise into a chair, and said, "Sit here, no further do-dah from you!"

Madame entered the room again, saying, "Well, now we have a set of them. Why did you bring the girl here?"

Vickie said in reply, "Elise told the troopers that I was the one who picked up MacGregor and took him away. She is a witness."

Madame was beginning to feel uncomfortable with the situation. Things were getting complicated. She said, "Vickie, the more involvement that you make in this mess, the harder it will go on you. Now you have kidnapped two persons, and I am holding them here against their will. This could get very sticky."

Madame went to the hot line and placed a call to Bud Hardwicke. She was counting the rings as usual, five of them, until Bud would answer.

Madame said, "Bud, we have two hostages here at your command. What are we to do with them? You have to remember that they are being held here against their will. Elise was the witness to Ian's disappearance and she has told the State Police that she saw it happen."

Bud was sputtering a bit, but managed to say, "My dear Madame, you are to be a gracious host to them. Do not be belligerent or overbearing. I am in talks with the padre and I plan to prevail in them. I will speak to you later in the day. Good bye."

Momentarily, the phone rang, and Madame answered.

The caller voice said, "Good morning Madame, Henry Horton here. I hope that the beautiful clear warm morning brings you a delightful day. A day that you will not make many phone calls tying up our lines. Please be considerate, Madame."

Madame felt that Henry Horton was about to make the camel fall down. Madame said, "Horton, you jerk, I will make as many calls as I want to and you know that I pay for each of them without question."

Henry was smiling to himself, as he hit the intended nerve once again. He said, "I just thought that you might consider being nice to others for once, good day to you, Madame."

Madame hung up. The expression on her face was priceless, as she was seriously cranked at Mr. Horton. Madame turned to speak to Elise, as Bud had directed, "Elise, have you had your breakfast this morning?"

Elise was continuing the struggle, and said, "Yes, I have, what is it to you anyway?"

Madame added, "Young lady, you will just have to hack it here until some events develop. So, calm down, and it won't be so bad."

Elise snapped back at Madame, and said, "If you say so, fat one!"

Madame grinned and replied, "Insults will not benefit you, young woman. MacGregor here, has been insulting me for the last two days without success."

The phone rang at the rectory of St. Jerome's parish. It was determined that the call was for Father Bill.

"Father Bill," the caller's voice said, "This is Bud Hardwicke. I'm calling in response to the disappearance of Ian and Elise. This is the second day of their confinement. Only twenty-four hours remain before they will be sent away. The terms are simple. You are to cancel the remaining parish raffles, forever, and you are to leave town immediately. Upon confirmation of this, the kids will be released, unharmed. Do you understand?"

Bill was amazed that he, himself was being pushed into this delicate situation by an old codger who won't let go of his sins or his crimes.

Bill said, "Mr. Hardwicke, I have no intention of granting your demands. Let me point out that you have overstepped your bounds with kidnapping. Kidnapping has been a Federal Crime ever since the Lindberg case. Punishments can extend to life imprisonment, or even execution. The actual kidnapping was done by Vickie. However, it was at your direction. Ian and Elise are being held captive against their wills."

Bud continued, "You have come here to Antrim Junction and with all your holy efforts you have brought ruin to me. Things have been peaceful here for me for many years. I am not going to sit by and let it happen without a fight."

Bill added, "Bud, I can't over emphasize the gravity of the situation that you have created. The State Police will be in town tomorrow afternoon. It is expected that this will bring down Dudley as Chief and Vickie's boss. The trail from Dudley will lead them directly to you. Think about it, Bud, and call me back in a few hours. Good bye."

Bill hung up. He was thinking about what he had said to Bud. He was trying to decide if he had placed Ian and Elise into a higher level of danger. Still in deep thought, Bill heard a voice. It belonged to Joe Williams.

Father Joe said, "What is the latest, Bill?"

Bill replied, "Joe, that call was from Bud Hardwicke. He demands that we cancel all future parish raffles and that I leave town immediately. I told him that he has gone too far with two kidnappings and he could go to jail for the rest of his life. Kidnapping is a Federal Crime."

Joe asked, "What is your plan?"

Bill answered, "I haven't got a plan. But with the lecture I gave him, he should re-consider his actions. At any rate, he will be calling me back in a few hours. In the meantime, we are watching Madame's house. The slightest appearance of anything unusual will bring in a raid by the State Police troopers. The warrants are not from Judge Stewart. They are from a Federal Judge. They are sort of an all-purpose warrant."

Joe's voice became the voice of a concerned pastor, "Bill, you must assure me that every effort is taken to keep the kids from getting hurt. If a rescue effort is mounted, keep violence to a minimum. Neither Vickie or Madame could out run an ant, but they could fall on you!"

Bill said, "Joe, no one knows better than I do as to how grave this situation can get. If either of these kids gets hurt, it will not do anything but put Bud, Dudley, Madame, and Vickie in jail for a long, long time. I am personally going to take the first watch on Madame's house. I have my cell phone and I will call the troopers if I see any of the Hardwickes at the site."

Joe added, "Just be careful, Bill. We can't lose our curate over this matter either. You are not going anywhere. I must, however, brief Joe Sullivan about the developments. It was his final decision that brought you here to Antrim Junction, and one that I believe was inspired."

# Chapter 27

# *"A Big Change"*

Ian and Elise were kept in their confinement together. The togetherness gave them the time to get better acquainted. Ian said, "Elise, I am truly sorry that you have been dragged into this whole deal. It is true that it was not known just what these people would do if deprived of their ill gotten gains."

Elise answered, "Ian, I was quite upset after I saw Vickie take you away in the cop car. She has been getting progressively belligerent since the push to squash the numbers began. She's obviously running scared because she has willingly committed kidnapping not once, but twice. We are guests of the town phone freak and subject to her culinary distress."

"Elise," Ian said, "You will find that I have lost all respect for elders when it comes to these two tubs of lard who are holding us."

Elise smiled, and said, "Ian, I am praying for a reasonable outcome for us. I can't believe that Bud would go to this extreme to protect his stupid numbers and at the same time be so overt about it. How about Bart, do you think that he would hurt us?"

Ian said, "Elise, Bart has already been here to hassle me, just after I got into this room. He was here to announce that I am in an inescapable jam. I have been working Bart over verbally for the past two weeks. I have been telling him that this whole number thing could collapse, leaving him out in the cold. With no inherited job, he would actually have to get good grades and graduate into a fruitful kind of employment."

Ian continued, "I was making headway with him when this latest course of events took place. He was doing some deep thinking about his future, if the Bud Hardwicke regime were to evaporate. He has this ingrown character flaw when it comes to me wearing kilts. He mocks me by calling me skirt boy. He tries to collect a dollar a day fee to wear the kilt at school. He has the mistaken notion that he runs St. Jerome's High School. He has a pack of lackys who do his bidding and they flock around him so that they can receive titular approbation from him. This so called approval is of zero value, as you know."

Elise said, "Father Bill, in his comments, indicates that he has the utmost respect for you and your family, having come here from Scotland to start a new life. You came here on short notice and without many of your belongings. I have also seen that you won't back down from Bart, even coming to near fists in the hallway outside of the main office at school. You have sent Bart away from you in a maddened snit, while you stand back, just grinning at him."

Ian replied, "It does seem sporting of me that it riles him up so. At least it is quite a lot of fun. Bart could be a good kid, if he had some direction. He could benefit from some time spent with Father Bill. He has no respect for priests, which I suspect comes from his upbringing. If that could be overcome, Bart would be a good guy."

Before they knew it, it was noontime. Noise could be heard coming from the kitchen. Presently, Madame entered the confinement room.

Madame said, "It's time for lunch, jerks. I have prepared a culinary extravaganza for you. It is called peanut butter and jelly sandwiches, milk, and a fruit cup."

"Ta Dah." said Madame, while bringing in the tray with the food, "Now eat your meal pronto."

Madame left the room.

Ian said, "Elise, do you suppose that she would try to poison us with this stuff? I did, however, survive the oatmeal this morning. She is a fatso, so she has not missed many meals. Therefore, she can't be a bad cook."

Elise said, "We will see. At least we are not being held bound."

The kids proceeded to eat their lunch. It went on without event, and finally, Madame came in to collect the tray and the dishes. She exited the room and slammed the door shut. They could hear the lock close up outside.

The endless watch of the afternoon began with the end of their lunch. The afternoon wore on. Not much action was had until about 4 o'clock. Madame came into the room with a telephone. She plugged it into a jack. Madame set the phone on the table in front of Elise. Madame said, "Elise, call this number and speak to Father Bill. Tell him that you are OK and that you are being cared for."

Elise was perturbed at the order from Madame, and said, "What if I don't do it?"

Madame replied, "You will, if you know what is good for you."

Elise dialed the number. When the line answered, she said, "May I speak to Father Bill?"

In a few moments, Father Bill came onto the line and said, "Hello, this is Father Bill."

"Bill, this is Elise," Elise began her talk with Father Bill, being careful not to antagonize Madame while doing so. "I am calling to tell you that Ian and I are OK, and we are being cared for, including meals. Adamemay isway eingbay away erkjay elphay usway. Good bye, Bill."

Madame snatched up the telephone and left the room. She slammed the door shut and closed up the lock. Silence began again.

Ian was grinning at Elise, and said, "I did not catch what you said to Bill before you ended the call. What did you say?"

Elise smiled, and replied, "Ian, that was pig latin. I don't know if Bill or Madame caught it, but it meant, "Madame is being a jerk, help us."

"Pig latin is sometimes used by kids to converse with each other in the presence of their parents and other adults who can't figure it out. I'll teach it to you sometime."

It was now almost dark and with no sign of supper coming, Ian and Elise were wondering what was ahead for them tonight. Another half hour went by. It was nearly 7:30PM. Noises could be heard just outside the door. The door opened and Madame came into view along with Vickie. Vickie, for once, was not dressed as a cop. Vickie sat down and announced that supper would be in just a few minutes.

Vickie began her presentation, "Listen here, MacGregor, you are not in a very good spot. The padre is refusing our demands. This narrows the possible settlements to just a few options. You will eat your supper next, and mind you, you must decide a way out for yourselves. The only alternatives ahead will result in personal harm."

Ian responded, "Vickie, I have no intention of doing anything that will assist Bud Hardwicke. You can all go soak your heads."

Vickie started again, and said, "Elise, how about you, aren't you interested in solving your problem?"

Elise replied, "Vickie, I never had much respect for you being a Hardwicke puppet, and only having speed trap work to do. I have always wondered if you would ever know just what real police work is all about. You are just a fixture in Bud Hardwicke's master plan to fleece this county of its money, its self-respect, and its freedom. You'll get no help from me either."

Vickie said, "That does it, you two can't be helped. I can't be held responsible for what happens from here on out. Bud has an event planned for you later on today."

The supper consisted of some kind of beef stew like stuff, green beans, bread, milk, and a banana. Madame set up the meal for them. Madame said, "Eat up chumps, it's a long time till morning."

Madame and Vickie left the room and closed the lock up outside.

Ian said, "Elise, what do you think they will do to us? I don't like the tone of Madame's voice this time. I sense that she has had it with us, and Bud as well."

Elise added, "You may be right, Ian. Neither of us have been the least bit cordial to these people. They do not deserve good treatment. It will only be a short time before we find out what is up. This stew is pretty good, isn't that a surprise?"

Ian was slightly amused, and said, "What can you expect from a fat tub like Madame? She is, indeed, a strange person to deal with. She feels as though everyone should be impressed with her telephone expertise. Not many people are impressed with her. The first moment that I knew her was via insults in front of her house. This ugly yellow house must be haunted. It may be haunted by her."

Elise spoke again, "Madame has not been very far from her

house in many years according to my folks. It seems that as part of her participation in the "enterprises", the chauffeur always did her grocery shopping and brought everything here for her. By seeing her at the mailbox, you created a new event and managed to incite her many times over."

Ian said, "Yes, Elise, it is funny, and great fun as well, just like it is with Bart."

While the two of them were finishing up their evening meal, more sounds could be heard outside of the door. Suddenly, the door burst open and two men entered the confinement room. These guys had their faces obscured by what looked to be pantyhose pulled down over their heads. The one in charge said, "Stand up, you two."

Elise and Ian stood up as ordered. The kids were bound with their hands behind them and they were gagged. Then they were taken outside to a waiting vehicle. The two kids were placed in the rear seat of the car and then locked in. They were to settle in for a ride to some unknown destination.

The ride took about half an hour to forty-five minutes. It featured many, many turns so as to disorient the kids. After enduring a rough last few miles, the ride ended at what appeared to be a rustic cabin in some remote woods. They could not tell much about it as it was dark.

The doors of the car were opened for Ian and Elise and the captors ordered them to get out. They were hustled into the cabin in quite a rough manner. They were made to go completely inside where a cooler of food and drink was prepared for them. The kids were released from their bonds and then the gags were removed. After this unceremonious treatment, the thugs went outside, closed the padlock securely, and left the site. This turn of events left Ian and Elise alone locked in the cabin in the dark. After a time of grop-ing around inside the cabin, the two of them found that there were two sleeping bags here. They decided that they must settle down for the night. Since there were no lights, daylight would be needed to be a part of their escape plan.

## Chapter 28

# "Bart's Surprise"

When morning arrived, a bright sunrise was evident. Ian was looking out of the window and he could see the clear blue sky. He began to look around, but he could not tell where they are being held.

Ian spoke, "Elise, good morning, let's take a look at our situation. We're locked in a one room rustic cabin somewhere unknown. I can't recognize anything, do you?"

Elise was still showing the tireds, and after some more yawning, she said, "I think that we are somewhere near Torch Lake, judging by the trees."

"Then we must be about 35 miles or so from home." said Ian, "It would make sense since the ride was not an hour long. I suspect that all the turns were made for the purpose of confusing our sense of direction and thus mix us up as to where we were going."

Ian continued, "Let's see what there is to eat for breakfast. Ian looked through the stuff in the cooler and found some bacon, milk, ground beef, chip dip, four sodas, and some bananas. In a grocery bag next to the cooler was a box of frosted flakes, a bag of potato chips, a package of paper plates, some paper bowls, paper towels and some plastic utensils.

Ian said, "We can have frosted flakes and bananas for breakfast. Something tells me that our adventure will rachet up shortly, so we should eat right away."

Elise was now more awake, she said, "Yes, Ian, you are right. Since Bill is refusing their demands, we will, no doubt, be in for more jazz."

The two of them fixed their own breakfast and ate it while keeping a constant vigil out the window for the approach of the thugs. It was about another hour before any extraneous sounds were heard. Soon though, the quiet was broken by the loudness of the approaching thug mobile, obviously in need of a muffler. Ian supposed that it would be Bart who was coming to deliver the hassle. But it wasn't Bart. Instead the two thugs that were the main attraction the night before have returned.

They parked their car, got out, and proceeded to take several bags from the back seat. The two ill-reputes then came toward the cabin. Another moment later, the unlocking of the pad lock could be heard, with a loud definite click. The door flew open and the thugs entered.

The lead thug spoke, "Have you eaten your breakfast this morning? I actually don't care. However, the boss says to check."

Ian replied, "We have just finished frosted flakes and bananas. Who are you, anyway?"

The lead thug said, "We have an adventure for you. The boss says that Ian wears skirts to school, so you will now. Take off your clothes, now! The things that are in this bag are for you to wear, Mr. MacGregor. This includes your underwear. Get with it." He then turned to Elise, and said, "Since you want to be the great helper, you are to wear the clothes in this bag. This includes your underwear. Get with it! We will wait outside for you two. Make it snappy!"

Ian and Elise proceeded to change while keeping a hand on their personal modesty. Still, a glimpse of the other was hard to avoid. They began laughing at each other when it became clear that Ian was wearing a pink dress complete with Mary Jane shoes, white panty hose, and a pink sweater. Elise was dressed as Paul Bunyan, complete with suspenders and the appropriate stocking cap.

Time was moving on, so the thugs came back into the cabin to see why the kids were taking such a long time to dress.

The lead thug said, "Outside, now!"

It became clear that the two thugs were here to carry out some sort of hassle that was sure to embarrass both Ian and Elise. Thug #2 produced an electronic camera and he instructed the two kids to pose for photos. First, they were to stand side by side, followed by photos of each of them separately. While this was being done, thug #1 took the clothes that the kids were wearing. He bagged them up and placed the bags into the thug mobile. Another grocery bag was brought inside. In the bag were some items that could provide sustenance with the help of some cooking heat. A few matches and some kindling were furnished for use in the wood stove. There were pots and pans in the cabin that weren't noticed before. They could cook after a fashion for a supper of sorts. Also a camp light was furnished for lighting. After only a few more minutes, the thugs ordered Ian and Elise back into the cabin. The door was locked as before, and then the two thugs left.

Ian sat down, and said, "Well, wasn't that strange? I can't imagine just what a set of goofy photographs would profit those guys, or even Bud Hardwicke."

Elise spoke up, and said, "Ian, you must feel awfully silly dressed like that. It must be embarrassing. I think that they think that I am the Paul Bunyan person who always saves the day."

Ian smiled, "Don't worry about me, clothing is not a major issue here. This has been contrived so that proof can be made as to our safe condition. They took pictures of us to show others that they are furnishing us with discomfort. I guarantee that Father Bill will have those pictures in a few hours."

Elise, still being uneasy about this new situation, asked, "What shall we do now? Do we attempt to escape from this place? Where would we go? We don't know where we are at the moment."

Ian said, "Elise, I think that we should bide our time for a little while longer, just to see what's in store for us. There can't be anything worth causing harm to us. I think that Bud Hardwicke is beside himself trying to determine how to get out of this mess. After all, he is a party to kidnapping and he is the king of the numbers racket."

Later in the day, a phone call was placed to the rectory at St. Jerome parish. The caller asked for Father Bill.

When the caller heard Bill's voice, he said, "Out on your porch is a packet containing photographs of Ian and Elise. I would suggest that you look them over. They have been removed to a remote location. Time is running out, padre. You must act now!"

The caller hung up.

Father Bill immediately went to fetch the packet. He brought it inside so that he can have a close private took at it. In the packet Bill found four pictures. One of them showed Ian wearing a pink dress, one of Elise in a Paul Bunyan outfit, and two photos of them together. On the back of one of the photos was a note that read: "How would these two look tied to a railroad trestle?"

Father Bill was quite upset. He felt that he alone held the fate of the two kids in his hands. Bill telephoned the Michigan State Police. He asked for Sergeant Brown.

Bill said, "Sergeant Brown, this is Bill MacKenzie at St. Jerome's. I just received a packet of photographs from the kidnappers, and on the back of one of them it says that these two kids could soon be tied to a railroad trestle. I am feeling quite low at this turn of events, and at this point, I feel that I should give them what they want."

Sergeant Brown was quick with his response, and said, "No way, Father, we can't give in so easily. Ian, I feel would not go for it. I will be at your rectory within the hour. We will examine the photos, and we will try to determine where they were taken."

Bill replied, "OK Sergeant, I will be here."

Meanwhile, Ian and Elise were sitting in the cabin, wondering what lay ahead for them. There was very little to chuckle about.

Ian decided to speak, "Elise, I must admit that I did notice that you are a beautifully built, fine young woman, with everything in just the right place. I just thought that I should admit that."

Elise began, "Ian, I must also admit that I looked at you while you were naked and I noticed how well in shape you are. I have long admired a man who is in good shape. Then I had to snicker though, when I saw that the underwear that they gave you was a pink thong."

Ian was blushing, and said, "Well, yes, that was a surprise. Normally, a man in kilted uniform is dressed according to rule as long as he is not wearing underwear. That fact is rarely true for me. I always wondered how the Scots of history hacked it with the colder days, or even icy ones like here in Michigan. The thong is not a normal underwear in Scotland, however, it takes some getting used to."

Ian and Elise continued their small talk for a while.

Father Bill was sitting in his office, not paying much attention to anything in particular. He caught a whiff of a foul aroma. His memory had that smell stored for future reference. After a few moments, he recalled that the odor was that of Bishop Sullivan's cigars. Soon the good Bishop had entered Bill's office. Bill stood up in respect for his prelate.

Bill said, "Hello, Bishop Sullivan, this is a surprise to have you here today."

Bishop Joe began, "Sit down Bill. I am here to coach you regarding the two kidnapped kids from our school. I'm greatly grieved that the Hardwickes are behaving in this manner. They have evoked the ire of the Feds. Kidnapping is punishable by execution. These folks must cherish their numbers to such an extent that they would risk all to keep it."

Bill began, "Bishop, here are some photographs that were just received from the captors. Let me assure you that the fact that Ian is wearing a pink dress in no indication of who he is. This is a forced situation. I'm sure that the costumes represent a melodrama of sorts, one that would emulate an old time movie."

Bishop Joe smiled at the comments, and said, "Bill, I think that you are quite right. We have to formulate a plan to bring the kids back and to bring down the Hardwickes at the same time."

While the two priests were meeting, the sound of the doorbell could be heard. A few minutes later, the parish secretary came to the office door. The secretary said, "Fathers, Bart Hardwicke is here asking to meet with you."

Father Bill did not know how to react to this announcement, and so he asked Joe Sullivan, "Bishop, what shall we do?"

Bishop Joe immediately replied, "Show him into this office and bring in a chair for him. Bill, be ready for anything."

In a few minutes, Bart came into the office escorted by the par-ish secretary. He was shown a place to be seated.

Bill started, "Bart, this is Bishop Sullivan, the head of our dio-cese. He is here because of his concern for Ian and Elise. We were discussing our response to the latest call for a decision on our part as called for by the captors."

Bart began to speak, a definite un-Bart like tone was evident as Bart began, "Fathers, I am here to offer my help to solve this matter. Ian has been working me over for about two weeks, the subject of which was: "What was my future if and when the numbers racket collapsed?" I stormed away from him twice, leaving in a theatrical exit. Such did not impress Ian. I have been in deep thought about what he said, and about what has happened since. I can't overlook the kidnapping. It has made me sick to my stomach."

Bill asked, "What do you think can be done?"

Bart replied, "I believe that they have been taken to the hunting cabin in the Torch Lake area, and that they are being kept locked in."

Bill pulled out the photographs, and said, "Bart, look at these. Do any of the backgrounds look familiar?"

Bart examined the photos of Ian and Elise together, and grinned at the costumes. Bart's smile faded when he noticed something in the background.

Bart said, "This is the Torch Lake cabin. The unmistakable row of trash barrels are seen just behind Ian."

# Chapter 29

# *"The Rescue"*

Shortly, another person joined the meeting. It was Sergeant Brown of the Michigan State Police.

Sergeant Brown said, "Good afternoon, Fathers, and to you Bart. What has developed in the last hour?"

Bill answered, "Well, Bart has asked if he can help solve this dilemma. He has identified the location of the kid's captivity as a hunting cabin at Torch Lake. He is contrite as to his part in this series of events and he will help us as asked."

Sergeant Brown said, "It is a fine gesture, Bart. Ian and Elise are important members of this community. We must do all in our power to rescue them and to capture the perpetrators of the kidnapping. Bud Hardwicke is topmost on the list of targets for busting."

Bart began again, "It is definitely hard for me to go against granddad, however, this insanity must end, even if he has to go to jail. Someone could get hurt, or even killed. It just can't happen, not here."

Sergeant Brown continued, "Bart, I'm calling in a group of un-marked cars, and we'll need you to lead the head car to the cabin location. The other cars will come in after a few minutes, so as to not flush the culprits immediately. We will seek to release Ian and Elise and capture the kidnappers.

Bart said, "Yes, lets do it. The sooner that it happens, the better. As time goes on, these guys will get more brave."

It took half an hour for the cars to assemble in Antrim Junction. When all was in readiness, the caravan left town quietly, heading toward Torch lake. Meanwhile, at the cabin, Ian and Elise were getting testy as to what was to happen next.

Elise said, "Ian, what should we do? Should we break out the windows and leave, or shall we just wait?"

Ian replied, "Well, I think that we should know momentarily what the outcome is from those pictures that were sent to Father Bill. There is certainly a plan to rescue us, and soon."

Elise quipped, "I hope so."

Ian sensed that Elise was giving up hope on some sort of rescue effort. He said, "There is great concern for us and Bill won't settle for mediocre results. Don't forget that we have care for each other, that alone is valuable."

Elise smiled, and said, "Then let's smile about something. Who do you think that the two thugs are, really?"

Ian replied, "I think that they are two of the number couriers that are not in jail. Judging by their familiarity and by the way that they talk to each other. They are also quite familiar with the Bud Hardwicke regime. So, therefore, they will do his bidding regardless of the consequences."

While they were talking, they began to hear the noisy car approaching. They instantly knew that they were in for another round with the two thugs. Soon, the car came into view and it was pulled up almost to the porch this time.

The two ill-reputes got out of their car and came up onto the porch, opened the padlock and unlocked the door. They came in, and with much ado, ordered Ian and Elise to go outside.

Ian came out into the late afternoon sunshine and said, "What do you two jerks have in store for us today? Something, outrageous, no doubt."

Thug #1 said, "We will gather up your things into the bags. We are leaving this place. You're in for it now. Father Bill is not responding to our demands, regardless of the pictures that we sent to him."

Ian and Elise were loaded into the noisy car and then the four of them left the Torch Lake cabin site. It seemed to Ian that they were progressing towards the east. These guys were taking lots of turns, but the trend towards the east could be felt.

Only a few minutes had elapsed when the caravan of State Police cars arrived at the Torch Lake cabin. Bart opened his door first and ran up on the porch. He was surprised to find that the cabin was empty. Bart was likewise surprised that they were too late. Sergeant Brown took out his handi-talki and called out for air back up from a helicopter. A few minutes went by and then the distinctive sounds of a chopper could be heard. The chopper was probably standing by.

Sergeant Brown talked to the pilot. "There should be a lone car proceeding away from this location. Their tracks are only minutes old."

The pilot replied, "Roger, we saw a car going east from the site, making turns about every mile. It looks like the vehicle in question."

Sergeant Brown asked Bart, "What is their car like?"

Bart answered, "An older car, a noisy one that is in need of a muffler. It has a badly rusted roof and a dented in trunk lid."

Sergeant Brown relayed Bart's description to the pilot, who

then confirmed that they had spotted the car. Sergeant Brown's car was still several miles behind the kidnappers.

Ian and Elise began to torment the driver saying, "Did you ever earn a driver license? Did you see that a helicopter is following you? You may have installed yourselves into a substantial quantity of crap."

The driver, thug #1, now known as Brian, had not noticed the helicopter following him. He began to speed up, and was now driving mostly straight. Up ahead Ian could see a line of trees coming into view. This indicated that there was a stream of some sort near by. A sudden left turn was had, and then a fast right. Then the thug mobile came to a stop.

Brian said, "Get out you two jerks."

Brian was armed with a pistol and he was waving it around to indicate the direction that he wanted Ian and Elise to walk. Up ahead was a railroad trestle of the old Ann Arbor Railroad, now operated by a company who leases the line from the State of Michigan. Ian and Elise were ordered to walk down to the bottom of the trestle. Here they were tied to one of the wooden posts that formed the legs of the trestle. After binding the kids securely, the two thugs left.

Suddenly, the helicopter was on top of the whole scene. The two thugs, in their decrepit car scratched out in their own escape. Soon, several of the unmarked cars of the police caravan were on the chase. The chopper put down into the adjacent field by the railroad. Shortly, Sergeant Brown's unmarked car pulled up and Bart jumped out and ran down to the bottom of the trestle.

Ian was surprised to see Bart there with Sergeant Brown, and said, "Bart, what is this? How have you come here with the police?"

Bart began to untie the two captives, saying, "It's all your fault, Ian. I thought long and hard about what you said could happen if the numbers came to an end. Many of the consequences darted through my mind. I was wavering until the kidnapping happened. This event made me sick. I could not believe that granddad could stoop so low. I just could not let it go another round."

Bart continued, "Ian, I hope that this will help me out, although I will have punishment coming, it won't be so bad. I have it coming. Granddad has it coming. With luck, the whole machine can be exposed for what it is and then it can be put out of its misery. I am also still hearing Father Bill saying that the people of Antrim Junction are entitled to a new freedom from the numbers and the poverty that it brings."

Ian smiled and said, "Bart, I'm proud of you. My philosophy of life is to be who you are. I have always felt that you really are not the bully that was shown to me, instead, you could be a thoughtful guy, one who could stand up and be counted. This is why I always stood up to your efforts. I admit that I almost planted a fist in your face when you wanted a dollar for the privilege of wearing a kilt to school."

Bart grinned, "Yeah, Ian, you're right. It was just a front, and the crowd of guys around me were nothing more than lackys wanting Hardwicke approval for being jerks."

Elise said, "Bart, let's get on with the mopping up effort and collect the rest of the crooks."

Bart replied, "Let's do it."

The three of them got into Sergeant Brown's cop car, and as Sergeant Brown began to drive in the direction of Antrim Junction, he called in on the radio.

"Brown here, we need marked back up at the speed trap in

Antrim Junction, at Madame's house, the police station, and at the Bud Hardwicke residence."

Ian was surprised that they were going after the whole compliment of them yet today.

Ian said, "Sergeant Brown, to which one are we going?"

Sergeant Brown answered, "We are going to Madame's house. I believe that Vickie is probably there. Madame is the steering supervisor of the racket, and she will, no doubt, be in the know as to what has happened to the two thugs who held you at the Torch Lake cabin. They have been captured and are being transported to the Kalkaska Post for interrogation by our Post Commander and his assistant. When we get to Madame's house, you three will remain in the car, and I will do the thing with the fat blob."

When Sergeant Brown's cruiser reached Madame's residence, the group found that the house was all lit up. It was the brightest thing on the block. Inside, thanks to the lighting, they could see Madame walking about. Sergeant Brown was probably correct that Vickie was in her house.

Sergeant Brown went to the side door. This was where Ian and Elise entered and left from. He knocked very loudly on the door.

Sergeant Brown said, "Madame and Vickie, this is the State Police, I have warrants for your arrest for criminal kidnapping, kidnapping confinement, and participation in the numbers racket. Open up, Madame, or we will take down the door."

# Chapter 30

## *"Vickie and Madame"*

The silence from inside Madame's house was deafening. Finally, as an additional State car pulled up in front of the ugly yellow house, Madame opened the door.

Madame said, "What do you want, copper?"

Sergeant Brown smiled, as he thought that Madame was trying out for a part in a movie with her reply. He said, "You, Madame, are under arrest for kidnapping, resulting confinement, and involvement in the numbers racket. You can come along peacefully or we can drag you out, your choice."

Madame replied, "OK, I'll go. It was bound to happen."

Sergeant Brown asked, "Madame, where is Vickie?"

Madame answered, "She is inside, but watch out, she's in quite a stupor. She has eaten so much that she's incapacitated at the moment. You might have to haul her away on a stake truck."

Sergeant Brown handed the custody of Madame over to another officer, who proceeded to take her to the squad car and lock her into the back seat. Sergeant Brown entered Madame's house to look for Vickie. He noticed the dump atmosphere of the home. He could hear Vickie moaning in the far room. Ahead, he found the door ajar, where the moaning was louder. Upon opening the door, Sergeant Brown was stunned to see Vickie on a low couch, completely out of it.

Sergeant Brown said, "Vickie, what's happened? Are you drunk?"

Vickie moaned, "Drunk would be easy. This is an overeating stupor and I can't even move about."

Sergeant Brown called out on his handi-talki for a van and some medics to give assistance to Vickie.

Sergeant Brown said, "Vickie, I have to inform you that you are under arrest for kidnapping, confinement, and participation in the numbers racket. The medics will be here soon, and they will get you ready to be taken to Kalkaska for interrogation."

Sergeant Brown called the Post Commander for an update. The Post Commander said, "Brown, I have notified the Sheriff that a bumper crop of prisoners is heading his way, including two fat females."

Sergeant Brown said, "Sir, the Vickie cop character is presently in an overeating stupor. She can hardly move. We have called medics in to prepare her to come to the post. She will be transported in a van. She is the one that picked up Ian initially."

Sergeant Brown ended his chat with his boss and then turned his attention to Vickie. The medics were here to begin treating Vickie.

The lead medic said, "Sergeant Brown, this is the worst such stupor that I have ever seen. She needs to be taken to the hospital in Traverse City, the Munson Medical Center, Trauma division. You will have to arrange guarded security for her there."

Sergeant Brown grimaced, "OK, the Post Commander will have to tend to that. I will inform him of the change of plans."

Sergeant Brown advised the Post Commander that Vickie had

to be transported to Munson Medical Center for trauma treatment and that they would need security guarding her.

Later, after Madame and Vickie were on their respective ways to separate destinations, Sergeant Brown drove his cruiser over to the Bud Hardwicke residence. The three kids were still in place in the car. Several State Police cars were lined up in front of Bud's house. Sergeant Brown began looking for the Sergeant of the Watch, and found that Lt. Hawkins was in charge.

Sergeant Brown said, "What has developed, sir?"

Lt. Hawkins replied, "Well, Brown, Bud Hardwicke is holed up in his house and he is refusing contact. When we try to approach the porch, he shoots paint balls at us. Several of the troopers are covered with mauve paint. We've telephoned him and he says that we can take a flying leap at the moon. Perhaps Ian could call him and reason with him. Do you think that he could try?"

Sergeant Brown walked over to his squad car and stooped down to talk to Ian. Brown said, "Ian, Lt. Hawkins would like you to consider calling Bud on the telephone and to reason with him. What do you think?"

Ian answered, "Yes, Sergeant Brown, I would be happy to help, and perhaps Bart would want to talk to his granddad. Do you have the number, so that we can do it now?"

Sergeant Brown replied, "Yes we do. We can return to Madame's house where we can use her phone center, and you can call him from a familiar number. Then Bart can follow up with some family talk with Bud."

The four of them returned to Madame's house and went directly to her phone center. Ian sat down at the call director console and found that Bud's number, the hot line, was labeled. Ian picked up the handset, and pushed the Bud button. The telephone automatically dialed up Bud's number.

After five rings, Bud answered, "Hello, my dear Madame."

The caller said, "Mr. Hardwicke, this is Ian MacGregor. I'm calling from Madame's phone center. She has been arrested and taken away to the State Police Post in Kalkaska. She will eventually be handed over to the Sheriff for lodging. Vickie is under arrest. However, she has been taken to the Munson Medical Center in Traverse City for trauma treatment."

"Mr. Hardwicke, it's time for you to consider giving up. You can't keep on shooting the State troopers with paintballs. How juvenile of you."

Bud replied, "Hrumpffh, Ian, I once thought that I could trust that you would mind your own business as long as I minded mine. I guess that is not now the case. The two couriers who took you and the girl to Torch Lake and to the trestle have gone to jail. What you do not understand is that there are members of the numbers machine above me who are now calling the shots. They will be violent."

Ian began again, "Mr. Hardwicke, the best foot forward is to come out and assist the police in breaking this foothold. Do it now. I'm handing the telephone to another person to talk to you."

Bart took the telephone from Ian, and said, "Granddad? It's Bart. I love you pa. I can't let you go this easily. Come out and help us to end this nightmare, please. We are counting on you. Don't let your bullheaded Irish attitude blind you to what is right."

Bud answered Bart, and said, "Bart, you're a good kid, and you can be great in adulthood. I don't know how to move from here. These guys could kill me in the blink of a gnat's eye. I must think about what you and Ian have asked me to do. I will call the hot line back in a few minutes. Hold off the cops for now."

# Chapter 31
## *"Standoff At The Hardwickes"*

After Bud hung up, Ian turned to the others and said, "Do you think that he will do what's right? I think that he will. But, Sergeant Brown, you and your men will have to protect him if he bolts from the house. There are others who care calling the shots. He is just the visible pawn for the higher ups."

Sergeant Brown was delighted at hearing what Ian had found out from Bud, and he said, "Ian that's great. You found out info that could significantly change our situation at Bud's house. It will make handling this case a lot easier. Being just a pawn will ease up on his jail time. Getting the crime bosses will be the important focus now. I will advise the Post Commander as to this turn of events. Excuse me."

Sergeant Brown left the room, leaving the three kids by themselves. Bart said, "I am so concerned that granddad will go down for some big wig for doing his part in the big picture. I would go to jail for him if it would help. You see, I love him."

Ian smiled, and said, "Bart, I'm seeing a side of you that most folks do not know even existed. You, unlike many celtic men, have adult emotions. Congratulations. Father Bill's upbringing was without male emotion, and he has described his father to me as the great stone face. He feels it left a pit in his personal makeup."

Bart replied, "It shows, doesn't it?"

Elise spoke up, "For many adult males in this town, old time conditioning told them that they had to stand up and not be emotional. They needed to show the world that they are strong people. There are lots of them in Antrim Junction. My dad is one of them. It is a rare event if the slightest tear comes to his eyes."

Bart continued, "Ian, I have you to thank for this breakthrough. Maybe granddad will survive this. I sense that you're not concerned that you're still wearing a pink dress. The situation at hand is more important to you than your attire."

Ian smiled, and said, "I had lost track of the clothing issue, and, as I told Elise at the cabin, it is the least of my worries."

While they were talking, Andrew MacGregor came into the room. Andrew said, "Ian, you're alright. Thanks to God. And you, Elise, are likewise OK?"

The three kids agreed to Mr. MacGregor that they were fine.

Ian spoke up, "Father, this is Bart Hardwick, whose granddad is the heart of the visible numbers racket here in town. As it turns out, he is only a pawn for a larger organized crime machine. Sergeant Brown is attempting to rescue him before harm comes to him."

Andrew continued, "Ian, have you considered changing your clothes? You are cute in pink, but it doesn't match your macho image."

Ian replied, "I will, father, as soon as the situation here has backed off."

Sergeant Brown re-entered the room and said, "Folks, the situation at the Hardwicke residence is being escalated with gunfire directed at our officers. The kids will need to go back to the caretaker's house with you, Mr. MacGregor. Keep them there safely while we attempt to rescue Bud. The picture has definitely changed in just a short time. Some of the big guys are in the house and they have gunmen in there."

The kids stood up, and then Ian said, "Let's go home, father, and let the troopers do their work." The four of them moved to the door and began to walk east on Elm Street toward the service drive.

As they were walking, Ian said, "Father, where is Eric? I haven't seen him in a long time, since before I was kidnapped."

Andrew replied, "Ian, I don't know. I have not seen him either. He has not slept at home for three days, and as you know, he is an independent butthead, and there is no telling what he thinks is OK."

Suddenly, Ian noticed that Sergeant Brown's police cruiser was approaching the group. The car pulled up to the four walkers. Sergeant Brown said, "Mr. MacGregor, may I speak with you, it's urgent."

Andrew froze in his tracks and turned his attention immediately to Sergeant Brown. Andrew said, "Yes, Sergeant, what is it?"

Sergeant Brown began to speak to Andrew, "Sir, your son, Eric, is inside of Bud's house. He's the new hostage. We believe that Eric was delivering some food when he was taken. Now, a fellow named Lou is calling the shots and he has informed us that he will kill Eric and Bud if we do not leave immediately."

"We have," Sergeant Brown continued, "Pulled back some 500 feet to give them some room, but we cannot be sure of the safety of Eric and Bud."

Ian walked up and immediately recognized the look on his father's face. He knew that something was seriously wrong. Ian asked, "What's wrong?"

Andrew stood tall, and said, "Eric is a hostage in Bud's house and he is being held there by one of the higher ups of the crime family. He is being kept there at gun point. His life has been threatened as well as the life of Mr. Hardwicke."

Ian was astonished at this turn of events, and said, "We have to rescue him and Bud, like right now!"

When they got back to the caretaker's house, the three kids sat at the kitchen table. It seemed natural to go there as they did most of their family planning at that table.

Ian said, "Bart, what can you tell us about Bud's house that may be unusual, like a way to get inside, unnoticed?"

Bart thought for a moment, and said, "Ian, there is a walkout in the back and next to it is a dumb waiter that opens up outside. The chauffeur always brought the groceries to the back and sent them up in the dumb waiter. The only way to get in would be to ride up in it. And, Ian, you are small enough to do it. I suggest that you change out of your favorite dress and change into something dark. Tights, maybe, to let you be agile. You will need it."

Ian asked, "Where is my marble bag? I'll need some sort of diversion."

Ian went to change his clothes. He came back dressed as Bart had suggested, completely in black with a dark navy blue stocking cap. Ian began to load his bag. Besides the marbles, he took his stash of firecrackers, an aerosol bottle of air freshener, a cigarette lighter, some small tomatoes, and a bottle of glue.

Ian asked Bart to go with him part of the way to help him get inside unnoticed. As they approached the Hardwicke residence, Bart pointed out the location of the dumb waiter and he coached Ian as to how to run the machine. Also important was to not be noticed by the troopers and Andrew MacGregor, who were at a slight disadvantage having pulled back to the 500 foot point. The two boys didn't hear anything as they approached.

Moving furtively ahead, their progress was slow, but deliberate. Finally, they reached a point where Bart would drop back. Ian moved ahead as unobtrusively as possible. When he got to the walkout, he located the dumb waiter. The pilot lights on the machine were lit, indicating that the machine was functional. Ian climbed aboard and pushed the button for the main floor, and then he quickly closed the door. Ian was now feeling the need for bravado as the slow moving dumb waiter rose to the main floor. The dumb waiter stopped at its destination. He stayed put in the car for a few minutes in case the noise of the machine had caused Lou to become curious. After about 5 minutes, Ian opened the door quietly. He looked about to determine how he could get into the rooms. Ian checked the layout and noticed that the action was centered in the living room area.

Ian listened briefly. He could hear a gravelly voice that he did not recognize. Then he discovered that the unknown voice was that of Lou.

Ian listened further as Lou said, "Bud, we can't overemphasize the importance of the numbers here in Antrim Junction. It supports lots of our efforts. You are in deep trouble this time, Bud. I have informed the State Police Sergeant in charge that we will kill you and Eric if they do not go away."

Bud replied, "Lou, you can't harm Eric. He was just here to deliver your stinking pizza. After all, he has nothing to do what-so-ever with all of this!"

Lou raised his voice, and said, "Bud, he is Ian's brother. He is wearing a name tag: Eric MacGregor. The MacGregors have been a pain in the dorsal fin since they got here."

Lou returned to the phone calling. He called Sergeant Brown

who was in charge outside. When he answered, Lou said, "Brown, just what is your intention here? We want this over."

Sergeant Brown replied, "Lou, if you surrender, it will go a lot easier on you. If you persist in standing off, then the consequences are yours, and yours alone."

All this time, Ian was lurking about in the shadows. He noticed that Lou had moved a distance from his gun. No other weapons were visible. Very quietly, Ian crept toward the gun. He snatched it up and then backed away slowly into the shadows again. When Ian got back to the dumb waiter, he dropped the gun down the shaft.

Ian crept back to where Bud and Eric were being held and he noticed that while Bud was not tied up, Eric was. Suddenly, Eric noticed that Ian was in the room. Eric was communicating with Ian by eye contact. All of them realized that Lou was occupied on the telephone with Sergeant Brown. The possibility of releasing Eric was present, but only for a moment, as Lou's call was wrapping up. Eric's legs were untied, and then Ian had to retreat into the shadows once again.

Lou came back into the room, and said, "Bud, how can we get out of here?"

Bud replied in a sarcastic manner, "Walk out the front door with your arms in the air. Sergeant Brown will welcome your initiative."

Momentarily, the hot line rang that was next to Bud's easy chair. Bud answered the phone saying, "Hello, this is Bud."

The caller said, "Granddad, Bart here. Can anyone hear me in the room?"

Bud answered, "No."

Bart continued, "Granddad, Ian is in the house, and he is going to cause a commotion to flush Lou outside to possibly run from the police. If you understand, say OK. Ian is very brave to help you."

Bud said, "OK", and hung up.

Lou asked, "What was that call?"

Bud was being deceitful, and said, "It was the pizza place. They wanted to know if the food was OK. I said it was OK. They didn't, however, ask where their delivery man was. They will be calling the police about him very soon, and they will begin to look for their employee."

Lou just shrugged off the barb uttered by Bud. He then returned to the sitting room where he had been making telephone calls. Lou placed a call to Big Antoine.

When Tony answered, Lou said, "Tony, the State cops are still all around Bud's house. I have threatened to kill Bud and the pizza kid, who turns out to be the brother of the MacGregor kid. I have to make a move soon, or the cops will storm this house. They don't know that there is only one gun here. What do you want me to do?"

Big Tony replied, "Lou, you have to get out of there. Do what you can, minimize our losses, and get going!" Tony hung up.

Ian was smiling. Now he knew for sure that he had eliminated the only gun that was in Bud's house. This caused Ian's bravado to swell. He was ready to strike at Lou.

Lou stood up and began to walk back to the room where the hostages were being held. Part of the way there, Lou felt a stinging coldness hit the side of his face. It was a tomato.

Lou shouted, "What the heck!"

At this point, Ian jumped out into the open. He launched another tomato and scored another direct hit squarely on Lou's nose. Lou was clearly cranked. Lou was cranked because he realized that it was Ian MacGregor who was attacking him.

Ian shouted, "Well, Mister Big Shot, do you want some more? You are about to head to jail."

Ian ran down the service hallway, lighting firecrackers as he ran. He was causing much noise and confusion. He made the complete circle through the sitting room to the dining room and back. Ian launched another tomato at Lou. Smack! The sound of another direct hit.

Lou was quite mad at this turn of events. He decided to chase Ian down the hall. At this point, Ian decided to dump out about half of his marbles onto the floor. Lou did not notice the marbles and lost his footing and fell on his tail bone. The results of this fall was to inflict quite a lot of pain into Lou's back. This pause allowed Ian to come up behind Lou as he was trying to get back up on his feet. Ian took out the air freshener, and with his lighter, he lit the spray from the can on fire. This caused the creation of a 10 foot long blow torch. The torch flame caused Lou's hair to burn profusely.

Lou came up in a rage and tried to get at Ian, only to fall on more marbles. He fell against the door jamb, breaking his nose. Blood was pouring out of his nose as he regained his standing posture. He noticed that he was badly hurt since there was blood everywhere. Lou decided to go downstairs. He then bolted out the rear walkout to get to his car. He quickly started the car and sped off.

Ian ran out of the front door, and signaled to Sergeant Brown's men that Lou was on the run. Four of the five cars took off after Lou.

Ian went back into the house to untie Eric and check on Bud. As Sergeant Brown came in, he was amazed to see that all of the effort seen from the outside was the result of one person. He surmised that Ian MacGregor is a one person team of marauders.

Sergeant Brown said, "Ian, we saw flashes of light, heard a lot of noise, saw a blow torch go off, and then Lou came out on a run."

Ian managed a small smile, and said, "Sergeant, I think that it's evident that Mr. Hardwicke was being kept in the numbers racket against his will. I heard Lou on the telephone with someone whom he addressed as Big Tony."

Sergeant Brown replied, "Yes, I see the same thing. I will assure Bud that the details of these findings will be in my report to the prosecutors. But for now, all of us have to go to the Kalkaska Post for debriefing by our Post Commander and Lt. Hawkins."

# Chapter 32

# *"Eric Speaks"*

After the ordeal of debriefing at the State Police Post in Kalkaska, the four kids returned to the caretaker's house around 10PM. There they found Elise's parents, Andrew MacGregor, Father Bill, Father Joe and Bishop Sullivan.

Ian exclaimed, "Wow! What a reception committee we have here!"

Bishop Sullivan spoke up, "Ian, we are dumbfounded at your bravery, in the face of possible personal danger. Your efforts have saved lives, and have infused this community with a large dose of pride and freedom, unknown for many decades. Let me be the first to advise you of a community wide celebration next Wednesday. You are loved and admired."

Ian blushed, and said, "Father, I didn't think of anything like that when there was a need to break up the standoff. I just decided that it had to be done."

Father Bill interjected here, "Ian, you have shown me the way to be proud. I had the feeling that you would. You will see what you did next week."

Father Joe added, "Folks, I am free. One of the captives is on the loose. I could not feel better than I do at this moment. You will see me around town form now on."

Bart spoke up, "If you please, the affect of Ian MacGregor coming to Antrim Junction will long be remembered. He IS home. I am proud to know him. I will try to live up to what he always told me that I could."

Elise said, "I must be going home with my folks. I need to wind down. I will see you heroes tomorrow."

Father Bill said, "Folks, the second parish raffle is being drawn after the vigil Mass on Saturday. Let's get about promoting it tomorrow. Let's be a success with that too."

After the departure of Bart and Elise, Bishop Sullivan invited the priests and Ian to sit at the strategy table in the kitchen..

The Bishop said, "Father Bill, if you will remember, I sent you here to Antrim Junction as a sort of punishment following an antic filled career as a seminarian. In keeping with the terms of the assignment, for two years, I plan to announce a year of favor for St. Jerome's. This parish will anchor the area's parishes for collegiality, for fund raising, and for attention to the athletic needs of our grade school kids. It is these three things that are now yours to see to, Father Bill. You have exceeded my most sincere hope for success here, and you, with Ian's help, have shown the air of freedom for our beloved Father Joe Williams and the people of this really great town."

Bill began, "Bishop Sullivan, I am surprised that you feel that I am capable of handling this expansion of my assignment here. I welcome the challenge that you have placed before me sir. Thank you."

At this time, Ian spoke up, "Bishop Sullivan, we are pleased to have you in our parish any time that you can be here. The people of the parish were very happy to see you here when you presided at the vigil Mass on the weekend that we had the first raffle. Many wide, pleased grins were seen in the pews."

Bishop Sullivan replied, "Ian, once again you are right. I now realize that a visible presence is quite valuable to the operation of a diocese, and if the people see their Bishop, they will feel secure that the Catholic Church is their church. I should have taken example from the Bishop of Saginaw, who sold his Episcopal mansion, put the money in a trust fund, and lived out his life as Bishop as a resident of the various rectories of his diocese. He lived in each parish about six months at a time. The Saginaw parishioners knew their Bishop personally. I will take example from you and him in the future."

Bishop Sullivan continued, "Incidentally, Ian, I wanted to thank you for your kind initial welcome that morning that Vickie had pulled me over at the speed trap. I understand, now, why you had lost any respect for Vickie and for the person known as Madame."

Ian said, "Reverend Bishop, thank you, I hope to get to know you better. Scots and Irish can get along, just watch."

Bishop Sullivan added, "Father Joe, it must feel wonderful to be out in the free air, air that is really free. Many of your people have told me how much they love having you as their pastor."

At this time, the priests prepared to return to the rectory. This left the MacGregors together in the kitchen. Eric seemed to be choking a bit.

Eric said, "Ian, I can't tell you how much I admire your bravery, after all, you rescued myself and Mr. Hardwicke from a situation that could have harmed us or even killed us."

"I have always put you down as a little kid, who could not manage to accomplish anything of merit. You sized up the situation, and decided to effect a remedy yourself. Watching you handle Lou in Bud's house was quite a neat deal."

Ian replied, "Well, when I heard Lou tell Big Tony that there was only one gun in the house, I was then at ease to proceed. I was able to sneak in and take it when Lou was occupied on the telephone. I then dropped the gun down the dumb waiter shaft. At that point, Lou was at the mercy of the tomatoes that I took with me, and then the marbles put the icing on the cake. What have you heard about the capture of Lou? He scrammed out of the basement walkout and left in his car with some State Police cars in pursuit."

Eric answered, "Lou only got a few miles south of the IGA Store. The blood from his broken nose was distracting his driving, and he ran off the road and into a ditch. He was captured, unarmed, and was then taken to Kalkaska. He will soon be a guest of our County Sheriff."

Ian recognized that something was up with his father, and said, "Father, it's called emotions. Let me be the first to tell you that it is OK to have them. Traditionally, Scottish males are taught to be tough and un-smiling, to show no emotions, and to be, in modern terms, macho. If they were to have shown emotions, they were considered unmanly. It takes a big man to show us emotions, and still stand up and be a Scot. Be who you are." Ian hugged his father.

When Friday arrived, there was a lot of attention to the selling and buying of parish raffle tickets. The mood of the town's people was very upbeat, happy, and ready to help each other.

The winning raffle tickets would be drawn, as before, after the vigil Mass on Saturday evening. The proceeds from the raffle would be used for school purposes. This fact drives the smiles during the sales of the tickets. Another important point was that the town's folks were keeping in mind that the illegal numbers racket was now in the past. Also part of the past is speed trap Vickie, and Chief Dudley Hardwicke.

The celebration in the gym after Mass was in high gear well before the appointed time to draw the winners. As before, Father Bill announced that the winners had to be at least eighteen years of age or older.

Bill said, "We will draw the second prize first, followed by the first prize, then the third and fourth prizes.

The prizes were all won by very deserving persons, to the joy of the assembled crowd.

Father Bill said, "Thank you, all of you, for making this raffle a big success. See that the winners are going to benefit from their winnings, and see also that no one spent more than $10 on raffle tickets."

Bill continued, "This Wednesday, we will celebrate a Mass of Thanksgiving at St. Jerome's Church at 5PM. After the Mass, we will have a special awards ceremony for our home town heroes."

At this, the crowd cheered. They were, indeed, in a very good mood.

# Chapter 33

# *"A Surprising Outcome"*

The weekend went well. There were no upheavals in town at all. The peaceful spring weather brought a happiness of its own to Antrim Junction. While everyone was enjoying the peace, there were some of the locals who were unhappy. Among these unhappy persons, one could count Vickie and Madame Blimpneflah.

It was time to further interrogate Vickie about her role in the numbers racket. Lt. Hawkins, the assistant Post Commander at the State Police post in Kalkaska, was present to ask the questions.

Lt. Hawkins began, "Vickie, how is it that you had your job with the Antrim Junction Police Department? You have no police training, you do not have any law enforcement credentials, nor is there much record of your having completed high school."

Vickie began her answer, "Yes, sir, this is quite correct. I am a nobody when it comes to the record. I served the Hardwickes in a hassle capacity, whereby I stopped every car entering Antrim Junction that I didn't recognize. If I didn't recognize a driver, I stopped them. By doing so, I could advise the Hardwickes as to who was in town."

Lt. Hawkins asked another question, "Vickie, it seems that you stopped Sergeant Brown at your speed trap and furnished him with a dose of flack. Was there a reason to hassle a uniformed officer?"

Vickie replied, "Sir, that was my mission. To know who was here and to alert the Hardwickes. It was a car that I did not recognize, nor did I recognize the driver. Let me say that the MacGregor kid gave me as much hassle back as I gave him. He said that I should think about the consequences that would befall me if the numbers were to be no more."

Lt. Hawkins said, "Vickie, his name is Ian, and he should be addressed correctly. He gave you some really good advice, and so, I am thinking that you should be grateful that things didn't turn out any the worse than it did."

Vickie said, "Well, the kidnapping was the worst thing that I have ever done. It is therefore necessary to ask Ian and Elise for forgiveness. I do not deserve any. I will help the prosecution in their effort."

Lt. Hawkins took note of the sound of some repentance on Vickie's part.

Meanwhile, Sergeants Brown and Smith were at the Antrim Junction City Hall complex. They, along with three assistants, are ready to serve a delayed search warrant. The two sergeants requested the presence of Richard Leslie to witness on behalf of the City. One of the officers agreed to witness for the State of Michigan.

Mayor Leslie said, "Sergeants, what materials can we get for you that will comply with your warrant?"

Sergeant Brown replied, "We need all of the records that apply to Dudley Hardwicke and how he received council approval to be hired as the Chief of Police. Further, we need all documents that relate to Vickie being a patrol officer and how that came about."

Mayor Leslie answered, "Yes sir, coming right up. I have had my staff round up the stuff since you were last here in my office. We will not conceal anything from you whatsoever. I am in possession of the new good feeling in town and I am happy to help you."

Sergeants Brown and Smith were pleased that Mr. Leslie was being so cooperative. They gathered up the documents and prepared to leave.

Sergeant Brown said, "Mr. Leslie, thank you. You know, we are arresting Dudley as you and I are speaking. You will need to name the Sergeant of the Watch as the acting Chief. You will also have to convene an emergency meeting of the City Council in order to place on the official record that there is a need to hire a qualified Chief of Police. The Post Commander at Kalkaska can furnish the requirements to you if you are in need, or he can help you if clarifications are needed."

Richard Leslie breathed a sigh of relief as no problem seemed to be as a result of him personally. The Mayor said, "Thank you gentlemen, please call me if more is needed."

The two sergeants left City Hall to take the proceeds of the search warrant to the prosecutors office. It seems that that there is a need, more than ever before, for Antrim Junction to come into the present day world and as such they would have an organized city. As the Sergeants passed the speed trap, they saw a DPW crew removing the speed limit sign from the welcome sign. A new paint job will be done very soon.

Father Bill was walking over to Mooney's, accompanied by Father Joe Williams. When they entered the shop, they purchased their intended treat, double dip vanilla cones. They saw Ian and Bart enjoying their double dip cones, so appropriate on a warm spring afternoon. Ian was grinning broadly when he saw the padres coming toward them.

As the padres sat down, Ian said, "Father Joe, welcome to the fresh world of Antrim Junction. I hope that it feels good to you."

Joe smiled, and said, "Ian, I have you and Bill to thank for this fine feeling. The people of this whole area are deeply grateful to the two of you as is Joe Sullivan. I have not found much success in this ministry here, but so many people have said to me: "Thanks for being here, we love you." Wow what a difference has come to the forefront since the numbers fell apart."

Bill said, "Well, Bart, what has happened to you as a result of this whole ordeal?"

Bart replied, "Father, Lt. Hawkins said that since I am still a juvenile, that I will not be charged with any crime. They will, however, petition me to probate court for behavior management. I can handle that. I have Ian to thank for the good outcome."

Bill added, "Bart, don't forget that you came forward to help, and attended a meeting at the rectory at which the Bishop participated. It all goes in your favor."

Ian asked, "What will happen to your granddad?"

Bart answered, "It is not yet known. But he will have to answer in court for working the racket, and due to his age, he could receive house arrest for a period of years. That is at least what the prosecutor has offered to him, after all they wanted and have nabbed Big Tony. It was with the help of Henry Horton that the number where Big Tony was called was retrieved from the memory at the phone company. It was traced as to address, and then the State Police in that area arrested him. He is in the Genesee County Jail in Flint at this time as a guest of the local Sheriff."

Bart continued, "As to Vickie, she is contrite as to her part in the whole mess and she is helping the prosecution. She has asked to speak to Elise and Ian. Ian and Elise will be notified by the Sergeants as to when that will occur."

Father Bill added, "I have been informed that the chauffeur, the four couriers, Lou, and Big Tony are the desired trophies that have been arrested. It was further determined that Bud was not the one who was shooting the troopers with paint balls, it was Lou. Bud was being kept confined to his easy chair, and across the room, Eric was tied to another chair. The rest is history."

Ian spoke, "Folks, we can all rest easy that the numbers are gone. We can now get about helping each other make our way through our lives. Each of us, being who we are, needs to stand up and be just that, WHO WE ARE."

Joe Williams added, "Gee guys, this is a really neat treat. This ice cream is just up the street from the rectory. I know that I will probably gain some weight this summer on just ice cream cones."

Bill chimed in, "Joe, we will count on it. You are too skinny for a sixty year old man. You will also benefit from being outside and taking walks on a regular basis. We love you, Joe."

For another half hour the group of them basked in their new freedom. Soon, Elise entered Mooney's and joined them.

Elise smiled, and said, "How are all of you, especially you Father Joe?"

Joe grinned broadly, and said, "I am peachy fine!"

Bill reminded the group, "After the Mass of Thanksgiving, there will be a special award program in the gym. So, I suggest that all of you rehearse your ad-libs. Several important persons will attend, so be appropriately surprised."

So ended a peaceful afternoon at Mooney's. Fathers Joe and Bill left Mooney's and walked north along Main Street, an effort that Joe had not done in many years. Upon arrival at the corner of

Main and Elm, the priests turned right and began to head east. Up ahead was the ugly yellow house. They proceeded to deliberately walk past Madame's house. When they were directly in front of the mailbox, an uproar was heard from inside.

"Stop where you are, holy Joes!", shouted Madame from the gaudy house.

Another normal sight came suddenly as Madame burst forth from the house and came directly out to the sidewalk. Madame said, "Hello, Fathers, are you out for a walk in the free air?"

Bill, at first rolled his eyes up to the clouds, and then said, "Yes, Madame, we are indeed enjoying this lovely afternoon. And you?"

Madame smiled at Bill for the first time ever, and said, "Yes, I am. I have you and Ian to thank for the new freedom here in Antrim Junction, and yes, even here in my tattered old house. I'm having it painted. The yellow goes. I had felt trapped with the numbers for a long, long time. I have been charged with misdemeanor confinement, and I have paid a fine. I also must perform community service of 85 hours. Judge Stewart is gone and we have a new judge courtesy of our good governor. I am asking you two if I may serve the community hours at St. Jerome's, possibly in the summer baseball program?"

Father Joe Williams was very pleased to hear Madame ask this question, and said, "Yes, Madame, we would be happy to comply, for forgiveness overflows at St. Jerome's."

The three of them chatted for a few more minutes and then the priests continued on their walk.

When Joe and Bill reached their rectory, they settled down for their evening meal. Joe said, "Bill, I am overwhelmed with the outcomes that we have witnessed just today. Madame was a complete surprise. She could actually be human."

# Chapter 34

# "The Big Celebration"

The time for the big celebration was nearing. Ian was able to take some time to pause and to examine just where the important things in his life stood. He decided that with only about two weeks left in the school year that he would finish the term in fine shape. Bart was at last a viable member of the student body. Elise was slowly overcoming the effects of the trauma from being kidnapped. Father Bill was becoming who he really is. Father Joe Williams is free at last. Ian's father was realizing how emotions are an important part of life, and Eric was actually being a real brother to him. What a list of accomplishments!

Ian was feeling good about everything. He needed to talk to someone. He was alone in the caretaker's house when he decided to call Elise. While the telephone was ringing, he was thinking of what to say.

The telephone answered, "Hello."

Ian said, "Hello, Elise?"

Elise replied, "Yes, Ian, this is Elise. How are you doing? It is that I am doing better, but some trauma effects keep coming back. The whole thing with the confinement is the problem."

Ian said, "Elise, I have been concerned for your well being since you left my house that evening. I'm OK, and many others involved in the whole ordeal are getting over it."

Elise added, "Ian I will be able to handle things by Wednesday. I hope that the celebration will go well. I have seen Father Joe walking about town with Father Bill and he seems happy for once. It is time to build on our new found happiness to make Antrim Junction a great place to live. It may just help the college, and all of the businesses here as well as helping to make a better standard of living here in our town."

Elise continued, "Ian, I am sure that we will see each other before the big day. I know that you'll be OK. You are the main hero and very brave."

Ian replied, "You sure know how to make me blush. I did what I had to save my brother and Mr. Hardwicke. After all, it turns out that Bud was just the local visible puppet, whose strings were being pulled by Big Tony. Once Lou let it be known that there was only one gun present besides the paint ball gun, I was able to dispatch the firearm down the dumbwaiter shaft. I was then able to let Lou have it with both barrels. The tomato pelting began the chase through the house followed by the marble roll in the hallway. That's where Lou broke his nose. He ran and was captured."

Elise answered, "Ian, it's important that all involved are safe. The blessings of the Christ are with us. We will live in freedom from now on. Oppression is behind us. The free air outside will permeate our souls and it will give new life to our resolve to move on."

Ian, as always, was surprised with Elise's ability to philosophize and said, "Elise, you have a profound way to say it and I think that we can simply say wow."

Elise came back and said, "Ian, I'll see you at school tomorrow, and we'll revisit this ordeal over lunch, OK?"

Ian answered, "Yes, it's a date."

The call ended just as Andrew MacGregor came into the room. Andrew said, "Ian, it is important to talk to the people in your life who were impacted by the numbers racket, so you can encourage them to move on and look forward to a bright future."

Ian replied, "Father, you are right to the penny. I have just been talking with Elise on the phone about just that subject. She is still experiencing some trauma from the kidnapping. The confinement keeps flashing back. I assured her that we were all in this together, and that we will prevail, and move on."

As Ian was talking with his father, Eric, came into the room. Eric seemed to be quite nervous.

`Finally, after several minutes, Eric spoke, "Ian, I do not have the right words to say to you. I have been a jerk of a brother to you. Even when you were trying to snap me out of my doldrums. I snapped back at you and put you down. Now, I have my life to live, thanks to you. I can't thank you enough for showing me bravery that I never thought existed in our family."

Ian was surprised by what Eric was saying. He replied, "Eric, I did what had to be done. As it turned out, Lou was more bark than bite, and a little kid beat him at his own game. He ran and was captured. Plus Big Tony was nabbed and he is in the Genesee County Jail at this time. He won't see daylight for a long time."

Eric answered, "Ian is it a happy ending or is it a happy beginning?"

Ian smiled, and said, "Eric, it is a happy beginning. The future is bright here in Antrim Junction. Even Father Joe is out and about the town these days. What a joyful feeling is being enjoyed among the people here. Here's an idea, let's have a big family style picnic after the awards ceremony on Wednesday. What do you think?"

Andrew spoke up at this time, "Ian, you psychic, it's already planned for the picnic grove for about 7PM, and as you say, cool, isn't it?"

Tuesday morning went kind of slow for Ian. He was looking forward to seeing Elise at the noon break. When the bell rang to signal the end of fourth hour, Ian was ready to head to the lunch room. After he got his tray, he found Elise and sat down.

Ian said, "Hi, how are you this fine day?"

Elise was smiling broadly, and said, "Hi, Ian, I am much better, and thanks for the encouraging phone call last night. This morning went well, with classes, as I have just two remaining courses to finish. The rest of the day I spend in the office where I do filing, typing, and whatever else is needed. By the way, the principal, Mr. Kelley has had a change of heart about keeping his job. He is really acting like a stringless principal. How amazing."

Ian smiled, and said, "I am pleased. I used to think that Bart ran him just as easily as Bud ran the town. The whole picture has changed. All of those reprobates are in jail, including Vickie. Madame is going to be doing 85 hours of community service at St. Jerome's in the summer sports program for the grade school kids. Father Joe has accepted her offer. In the long run, I think that Madame will be an asset to our community. We will just have to train her properly."

Elise smiled. She noticed that the time for the noon break was running out. She said, "Hurry up, Ian, time is almost up for the break."

Ian replied, "OK I will see you later."

Wednesday dawned as a wonderfully clear day. A light warm breeze was blowing in from the southwest, and in general, the whole of Antrim Junction was awash with pride. After school, the four young ones were to gather at the caretaker's house to prepare to go to Mass.

Ian was ready early. He was wearing his beloved MacGregor kilt, a white dress shirt with a black tie, and of course sneakers with the tall cream colored kilt hose complete with red flashes. Soon, Ian heard a knock at the door. When he opened it, he was taken by surprise. There was Bart Hardwicke, dressed in, of all things, an Irish kilt of the county where the Hardwickes are from.

Ian exclaimed, "Wow, Bart, look at you! You can't be called non-skirt boy again! I am so happy for you. You can be who you are!"

Bart said, "It'll take a little getting used to but I agree that I must do this and not just this time, but every time an opportunity arises to be who I am, I will wear it. I am ready to be proud to be a Hardwicke, and an Irish Hardwicke to boot!"

Bart and Ian went into the caretaker's house and sat down in the kitchen. Within minutes Andrew and Eric came into the room. They too were dressed in their MacGregor tartans. Ian jumped for joy.

Ian yelled, "All right! You two are my prize for pride week. I am so pleased that your kilts are seeing daylight for the first time in years and for the first time in the US. Grandfather would be so happy for us."

Bart was smiling broadly at seeing Ian so happy. It was the culmination of a long road to show how life could be led.

Bart said, "The only one not here yet is Elise."

No sooner than Bart's words had cooled off a knock was heard at the door. It was Elise, right on time. Elise was dressed in a stunningly beautiful lavender velvet dress, and she was wearing a lovely hairdo. Her make up was well done, as always.

Elise said, "Hey everyone, are we ready to be regaled?"

Ian was still grinning and said, "Elise, you are a picture perfect young woman, a sight to behold. I hope that a photographic record can be had for this moment. We need to save the vision of you."

Elise was blushing. She said, "Ian, you could turn my head easily talking like that, Mr. Hero."

At 4:30, Andrew herded the young ones toward St. Jerome's church. As they entered the church, there was a round of applause for the kids and they were embarrassed over it. They sat in pews mid-way up the aisle. At 5:03PM the bells rang. The people stood up in respect for their priests, and looking toward the center aisle, the congregation could see the procession of priests and acolytes coming in to begin this special celebration. Leading the procession was Father Joe Williams, followed by Father William MacKenzie, and then Bishop Joe Sullivan. Also part of the procession were two lay readers of the Word, and some singers. Much to everyone's surprise, Father Joe was the principal presider. The Bishop sat back as a visiting priest would.

Father Joe announced, "Welcome to this special celebration. This Mass is being offered for the intention of Ian, Elise, Eric, Bart, their parents, their teachers and friends. Also, intention is made for this parish in thanksgiving for the recent blessings that the Lord, the Christ has showered upon us. Let us begin in the usual way, in the name of the +Father, and of the Son, and of their Holy Spirit, Amen."

The Mass proceeded in the usual way until it was time for the homily. At this time, Bishop Sullivan came forward to deliver the message.

Bishop Joe began, "My dear friends in the risen Christ, good afternoon. I am pleased to speak to you briefly today. Father Joe, your pastor and friend, is sixty years old. You would think that a man of that many years would be thinking about retirement, and of going fishing. He has said a firm no to that idea."

"Father Joe has asked to remain here as your pastor and he has asked that his work load remain constant. He indicates that the presence of a young curate here has made all the difference in the world to this parish. I have here a letter from the Holy Father, who writes, "Greetings from Rome to Father Joseph Williams, and to the people of St. Jerome's parish. I am pleased to announce to you and the faithful of your parish that I have decided to award you with a domestic prelature, and henceforth you will be addressed as Reverend Monsignor Joseph Williams. Congratulations, signed +John, Bishop of Rome."

At this announcement, the whole of the congregation broke into sustained applause for Father Joe. The applause lasted for several minutes. When the noise settled down, Father Joe rose from his seat and came forward to accept the document from his Bishop.

Bishop Sullivan continued, "Folks, we are grateful to Ian and his friends who have shown us the way to peace in this wonderful town. We owe them a debt of gratitude. I know each of you will be grateful in your own way. After the awards ceremony, there will be a picnic in the grove at the college, please try to attend. And now, let us continue our prayers together."

After Mass, Ian and Elise were looking at each other and smiled. Ian said, "Are you handling this?"

Elise, in agreement, said, "Yes, but just barely."

Ian said, "I will see you in the gym in 15 minutes."

Ian went into the sacristy where the priests were stowing their Mass vestments. Ian was in for the surprise of the month. There was Father Bill, dressed in his MacKenzie plaid. There couldn't have been a better surprise.

Ian said, "Bill, look at you. You look like who you are!! I am so pleased. This whole event has come full circle. At last this is home for me. I will never forget the kindness that you are showing right now. I will forever cherish this moment. Wow! Wow!"

Bill answered, "Ian, you have shown me the way. It was quite a hard road for me to do this. I have only worn this kilt once before today. I have explained my upbringing to you, and you understand how hard it is but, behold, I did it!"

Bishop Sullivan added, "I would have brought my own kilt if I had even thought about it. But, Irish as I am, we wear kilts, mostly single color, or county tartans."

"Excuse me folks," said Sergeant Brown who was at the door of the sacristy, "May I interrupt for a moment?"

Ian said, "Yes, sir, what can we do for you?"

Sergeant Brown replied, "I have Vickie outside. She would like to speak to you Ian and to Elise also. Could you consider a few moments for her?"

Ian was surprised, and said, "Yes, of course."

Ian walked out into the church along with Sergeant Brown to where Vickie was waiting. Elise came in from the side door.

The two kids were standing directly in front of Vickie.

Vickie said, "Ian, Elise, I have asked for some of your time to express to you how sorry I am for all that has happened. I have been a total jerk and do not deserve that you would talk to me. I am asking for your forgiveness for the kidnapping. I was completely wrong for it and I am prepared to be punished as the court will determine soon."

Ian was quite moved by Vickie's plea, and at the same time, Elise was puzzled by it.

Ian said, "I am pleased to forgive you, as I have learned from the

Christ, that judging is not mine to do, but for Him and the creator Father. May Christ's peace help you through your punishment."

Elise was stunned.

Elise spoke up, and said, "Vickie, you have made many lives miserable here in town for a long time, and you have assisted in the ruination of many families. Your affronts toward me were minimal as opposed to the others, but I too, will forgive you. And I suggest that your penance should include the folks that were involved. May Christ bless you."

Vickie thanked the two kids and then Sergeant Brown stepped forward to take Vickie back to the jail.

As Vickie was being taken away, the kids were looking at each other in amazement. Ian said, "I think that we did the right thing by forgiving her. She will have to pay the penalties that the court will impose. The kidnapping was an affront to society. We should visit her occasionally if she is imprisoned near here, or write to her if she is sent away."

Father Joe approached the two kids, and said, "Well, folks, we need to go to the gym for the ceremony, and then to the picnic grove for the ceremonial sacrificing of hot dogs."

At the gym, as folks were getting seated, the crowd noticed that Father Bill was dressed as a Scot, and at 6:55PM he received a round of applause for his duds.

When things settled down, Father Bill began to speak, "Gracious citizens of Antrim Junction, welcome. We are gathered here to thank Ian MacGregor for his tireless rescue of this community from the ravages of the numbers racket. He risked his life to rescue his brother Eric and to spare the life of Bud Hardwicke. Bud will be back in our community in about six months. We expect him to be sentenced to six months in the county jail followed by a period of house arrest. He will need loving, prayerful, support from a forgiving prayer family here. The higher ups, being Big Tony and Lou, will be guests of the State for about twenty years. Vickie is also expected to serve time in a Federal facility for the kidnapping charge. Madame Blimpneflah will be serving community service hours at St. Jerome's. Let's show these people that we can forgive and that we can share Christ with them too. Ian MacGregor, please come forward, along with Bart Hardwicke, Elise Leslie, and Eric MacGregor."

The four of them came up and stood beside Father Bill.

Father Bill continued, "We are proud, Ian, to give you the key to the city and to our hearts. You ARE HOME. Your people will second the motion."

At this the crowd broke into applause. This lasted for many minutes.

Ian stepped forward to speak, "My friends, thank you for this award, I will treasure it all of my life. I wanted to feel at home here ever since I first arrived from Scotland. I was made to come here, not knowing what lies ahead. With much learning, we did prevail in freeing Antrim Junction from the numbers, and our efforts also freed many families from the betting disease."

"Additionally, our efforts have changed the lives of many of the people that were directly involved with numbers. I am referring to Madame, Vickie, and Mr. Hardwicke. Of course, the big winner is Father Joe who is now free to be the kind of priest that he always dreamed that he could be."

Ian was searching for more to say when he heard a commotion to his right. Ian turned and saw a young man dressed in a bright yellow kilt. He immediately knew that this was the MacLeod tartan. It was Kevin!

Ian yelled, "Kevin!! Come here. Folks this is my life long pal from Scotland who is here for a visit, just arrived. I have missed him so. Please welcome him to our Scotland away from home."

The crowd responded in kind for Kevin. The two pals hugged each other.

Author Note:
Ian MacGregor is who I wanted John Paul to be.
John, you can be who you are!

# Author Biography

Name: James McCarthy
Born 4 June, 1946 in Flint, Michigan

Father: Frederick Alvin McCarthy

Mother: Eleanor Kathleen McCarthy

Heritage: Celtic. My Father's mother was born in Arbroath, Scotland, and came to the United States when she was around 10 years old. She married Joseph Jeremiah McCarthy in Massachusetts.

My mother's father was Albert Wesley Scott, son of Ransom Wesley Scott, her mother was Ane Louise Scott, nee: Hansen. She was of Danish descent, while Albert was of Scottish and American Indian descent.

Author's Education: Flushing Community School, Flushing, Michigan, graduating from their high school in 1964. Attended Mott Community College, Flint, Michigan, graduated with Associates Degree in Applied Sciences, Electronic Communication, 1967. The same year, obtained FCC first class radiotelephone operator's license, and State of Michigan electrical journeyman license.

Work History: McCarthy Electric, worked for father until began working at AM1470 WKMF, Flint. After a summer stint in radio, began working at WKNX-TV25 Saginaw, MI for 2 ½ years, then returned to WKMF for 9 more years. I managed the technical operation for WGMZ-FM which the company acquired in 1973. Downsizing took these jobs and I then went into business for myself as an electrical contractor.

Family: Married in 1971, we gave birth to three children 2 boys 1 girl, We adopted a girl in 1978 and raised three more girls to adulthood, a total of 7 children. Divorced in 1987.

Continued to raise the children and work work work. In the late 1980's I was accepted into the training program for the Western Orthodox Church in America, and was ordained a priest in 1991.

The last of the children left home in about 1994. I became associated with Emmanuel Catholic Church in Saginaw, MI as an associate pastor. I wrote "Ian and the Padre" during the recovery time from a total knee replacement surgery, being confined to quarters most of the time.

"Ian and the Padre" was built on a set of chapters that I had written as an exploratory several years ago, I re-read what I had written, and still liked it, and so I started over, with the first chapter is mostly like that which was filed away for years.

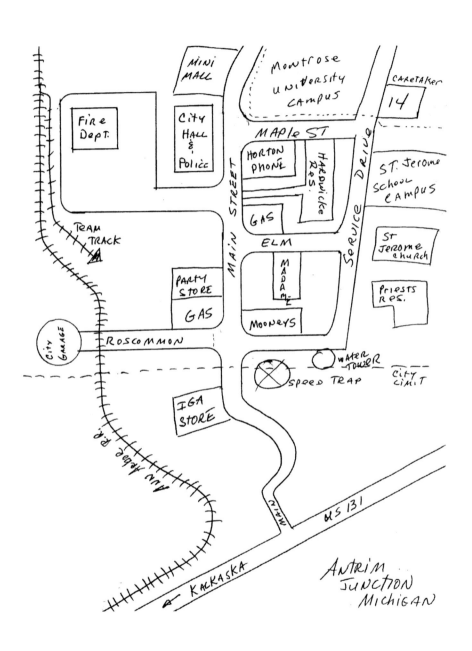

LaVergne, TN USA
31 March 2010
177706LV00003B/22/P